# CHANCING FAITH

## LARGE PRINT

By

Empi Baryeh

## A BLACK OPAL BOOKS
## PUBLICATION

GENRE: CONTEMPORARY RO-
MANCE/INTERRACIAL ROMANCE

CHANCING FAITH ~ Large Print
Copyright © 2012 by Empi Baryeh
All rights Reserved
Cover Design by Kimberly Killion
All cover art copyright © 2012 All Rights Reserved
LARGE PRINT ISBN: 978-1-626940-66-6
First Publication: MARCH 2012

http://www.blackopalbooks.com

**Thane knew he was in for it now. He could hardly believe he'd really done it...**

He'd kissed Naaki. *Kissed* her! What the hell was he thinking? Thane tossed his jacket aside and yanked off his tie. *Of all the stupid—*

Raking his fingers through his hair, he muttered a curse. The urge to hit something assaulted him with a force that should have surprised him. The perfect punching bag would have been his own body, since it was apparent that he needed to pound some sense into his skull. Right now, the only thing pounding was his heart as it threatened to burst out of his chest, throbbing partly out of anger but mostly from his pulsing desire.

Damned if he didn't still want her in his arms. She made him feel like a teenager— and not in a good way. Vulnerable wasn't a desired state of mind as far as he was concerned. He sat down with the adjoining door in full view, still unable to comprehend how he'd dropped his guard. How he seemed so *willing* to let down his defenses around her.

He'd panicked in the elevator, allowed himself to be captivated. He'd worried about her, touched her as if he cared. She'd kissed him back, moaned against his lips and his knees had gone weak. He could have made love to her right there in the lobby. He could *care* about her, and caring was the last thing he could afford to do.

*Dammit.* Naaki wasn't a woman you got involved with on a whim. He needed, at all cost, to avoid her—the woman who'd so easily brought him to his knees, who'd caused his body to come alive and made him want—

Just want.

**He didn't do short term relationships...**

American ad exec, Thane Aleksander, doesn't date co-workers either—until business takes him to Ghana, West Africa, and he meets Naaki. Now he's at risk of breaking all the rules. Can he stop this headlong fall before it's too late?

**Until he met her!**

Naaki Tabika has a burning need to prove, to herself and to others, that she's more than wife and mother material. To do so, she's prepared to give up everything for her job. Meeting Thane, however, makes her want to get personal. But falling for her boss could destroy her career. Will she be willing to risk it all for the one thing that can make her truly happy?

Two divergent cultures, two different races, two career-driven professionals, only one chance at true love—will they find the faith to take it, or will their hearts be sacrificed on the altar of financial success?

## KUDOS for *Chancing Faith*

*Chancing Faith* by Empi Baryeh is an enchanting interracial romance. Unlike some others I've read, this book isn't about color so much as interracial cultural differences. The story takes place in Ghana, Africa and has a nice foreign flavor to it that I quite enjoyed. Our hero, Thane, and our heroine, Naaki (he's American and White, she's African and Black) seem to be a good match and the conflict between them keeps the story interesting...the last thing Naaki wants to do is have an affair with the man in control of her career advancement. But being the hunk that Thane is, avoiding temptation is easier said than done. As far as Thane is concerned, Naaki is as exotic as her culture and the temptation to seduce her is even harder for him to resist...For a debut author, the book is very well done. – *Taylor, reviewer*

*Chancing Faith* by Empi Baryeh is a contemporary romance with a mix of cultural and business issues that make it an interesting read...the book has a unique foreign flavor, one of those stories that makes you want to curl up on the couch and immerse yourself in a different world—not just a different country, but a different culture. Baryeh managed to make the story easy to follow while keeping that feeling of being somewhere other than America. The food choices at the local restaurants, the spattering of foreign words, the dialogue of the African characters, and the potential threat of an American business taking over an African one and "Americanizing" it by forcing their policies and values on the employees, without regard to the culture those employees are living in, gives *Chancing Faith* a nice ring of truth. – *Regan, reviewer*

# DEDICATION

*Chancing Faith is dedicated to Max who inadvertently showed me that interracial relationships aren't always about color, to Ron who helped to ensure that Thane sounded American, to my family and friends, who have supported me since the very beginning, and to everyone who will read this book. I thank you all for making this worthwhile.*

# CHANCING FAITH

## LARGE PRINT

# CHAPTER 1

*Kotoka International airport, Accra, Ghana*:

The heat and the heaviness of the air stunned Thane Aleksander as he stepped off the Boeing seven-four-seven. *Whew*! He took a moment to readjust his breathing with the yoga exercises he tried to practice every now and then. He'd been briefed about his new country of residence, but nothing could have prepared him for the instant perspiration as he descended the vibrating airplane stairs.

He slung his laptop bag over his shoulders and slipped on his sunshades. Within minutes, his hair was damp, with beads of sweat congregating on his forehead and sideburns. His shirt clung to his skin. He grimaced, thinking of the sweat stains he'd have to take care of later on.

His business outside the US had so far been conducted in Europe and Asia, and he knew some adjustments would be necessary—not the least being the weather—but it was the humidity that was killing him.

Luckily, a shuttle arrived to transport passengers from the tarmac to the main airport building, but despite the air conditioning, the temperature inside didn't seem to be much of an improvement over the heat and humidity outside. He felt faint.

Entering the immigration hall, he scowled. There was only one counter for "Foreign Nationals?" He muttered an expletive and took a place in the queue. Had this been JFK, he'd have waltzed through with a "welcome home," from the customs officer.

But it wasn't America, he reminded himself. This was Africa, the place where, most local companies were considered to be either high-risk or incompetent. Until recently, only large consumer products manufacturers—who needed a global consumer base to remain profitable—had ventured into the territory. However, since attending an international advertising seminar in Egypt two years ago, Thane had been studying the market and tracking the exponential growth in the service industry here. If that trend continued—which he expected it to—in a decade, Africa would become the new China.

"Passport, please."

His turn. *Finally*. He handed over his passport.

The immigration officer, wearing an unflattering green uniform, scrutinized the document, flipped to the photo page, paused for a few seconds before looking up. "Why are you visiting Ghana?"

"Business." As stated in his visa—if the officer would read it.

The man nodded. "When are you leaving?"

*What the hell*? Talk about hostile. You'd think they intentionally hired obnoxious people to work in airports. Was there some international law that justified this kind of antagonism?

"I'll be here for six months."

The man scanned through the passport once more and finally settled on a fresh page. He stamped it and handed it back. "Welcome to Ghana."

Thane nodded and retrieved his passport.

Moments later, he stepped through the final exit and back into the prickling heat. It made him think of how much he'd like to take a dip, or at least, settle into his air-conditioned hotel suite as quickly as possible.

Casting a glance into the small crowd at the exit, he briefly registered emotional reunions and the eager looks of those still waiting for their loved ones to walk out. His gaze settled on a group of uniformed chauffeurs holding out large name cards. Those were the ones he was interested in, for he had no loved ones here. In fact, aside from his parents back home, he had no loved ones; period. And that was the way he intended to keep it.

He spotted his name, and an unexpected flush of relief flooded him.

"Mr. Alexander?" the man holding the card asked.

"Aleksander," Thane corrected. It was a common error, one he never seemed to get used to.

"*Akwaaba.* I'm here to take you to La Paulanda Hotel." The stocky chauffeur eagerly took charge of Thane's luggage.

The transport turned out to be a cozy minibus whose AC blasted cold air. Thane leaned back, sighing deeply. *Now that's what I'm talking about.* He made a mental check of his belongings: laptop, AC adapter, thumb drives, sunscreen, mosquito repellant, cortisone...nothing missing so far. Not that he'd expected otherwise, but the check was a calming down mechanism.

He didn't know why he felt more than a little nervous about being in Ghana. After all, it had been *his* idea to come here. Based on his recommendations, Black & Black, the advertising agency he worked for, had decided to expand their operations to Africa. Thane had been working with the agency as the International Account Director for five years now, a role that made him responsible for business development outside the US. He'd championed their expansion to Europe and Asia through affiliations with local agencies, personally handling the negotiations as he was about to do with Media Image Advertising—or MIA as it was commonly called—one of the largest advertising agencies in Ghana.

He'd negotiated plenty of deals with huge European companies and done business with many non-American organizations. Yet it seemed a daunting idea that he was here to do...pretty much what he did best. He attributed the attack of tension to this being his very first time in Sub-Saharan Africa.

His discomfort only increased when he arrived at the hotel and was informed by the reception desk that the presidential suite he'd reserved wasn't available. Briefly, he considered changing hotels. He wanted the larger accommodations in case he needed to hold meetings at the hotel, but he'd picked La Paulanda for its nearness to Media Image Advertising. Eventually, proximity and fatigue won out over space, and he accepted another suite—a much smaller one.

"Sir, if you'd like, I can check whether the presidential suite will become available during your stay at the hotel," the front desk clerk offered as she checked something on her computer screen. A frown settled on her features before she looked up. "Excuse me a moment, sir."

Picking up the phone, she made a call. She spoke in a local language, and even with several English words punctuating her sentences, it was impossible to decipher what she was saying.

Finally she hung up, giving him an apologetic smile. "Sorry, sir, the suite isn't going to be available for ten days, but if you really do need the space, there's an adjoining room to your suite, which is unoccupied. We can give both to you for the same rate as the presidential suite."

There was some logic in that. An extra room solved the problem of space, while providing some privacy. "I'll take it. Thank you."

The clerk answered him with a pleasant smile and handed him a key card. "*Akwaaba.*"

There was that word again. Since they said it with a smile, he assumed it meant something along the lines of "enjoy your stay." Not that it mattered. This wasn't a pleasure trip.

ৎ৯৫৩

When Thane called MIA office the next morning to announce his arrival in Ghana, he could feel their alarm right through the phone. The panic attack was understandable, he supposed. He was a week earlier than expected and would be making his first visit to them in just a few minutes.

He'd decided on a formal dress code despite the heat and cranked up the AC in the rented BMW. As the car eased to a smooth stop in front of the building, he ignored the curious stares he was attracting. All that mattered was his work and what lay ahead. The successful completion of this deal could be the determining factor in his making partner at Black & Black.

*Black, Black, & Aleksander.* A little long, but it had a nice ring to it. Having his name on one of the fastest growing advertising agencies in the US was a stepping-stone to becoming a major force in the industry.

Today, he planned to acquaint himself with the people at MIA, but mostly he wanted to go through the agency's files. He exited the car and walked into the building.

"Mr. Aleksander." The receptionist, her voice filled with panic-stricken awe, stood when he introduced himself. Fumbling with the intercom, she announced his arrival to Mr. Boateng, the acting managing director.

The short and plump man hurried into to the reception area, his arm extended. "Mr. Alexander."

"Aleksander," Thane corrected, giving the man's pudgy hand a shake.

"Yes." Mr. Boateng didn't seem to notice he was being corrected. "*Akwaaba.* 'Welcome' in English."

Thane smiled. "Thank you."

He followed Mr. Boateng into an office elaborately decorated in what he would previously have referred to as "African décor." After his one-night stay at the La Paulanda, however, Thane suspected the hand-carved ornaments and paintings were specifically indigenous to Ghana.

Talking to Mr. Boateng, and subsequently meeting the staff and familiarizing himself with the agency infrastructure, took nearly two hours, after which Thane retreated to his new office. Having asked not to be disturbed, he studied the company's files with an eye toward efficiency and productivity.

After three straight hours of work, exhaustion began to set in. It didn't help that his body was still functioning on Eastern Daylight Time. He sat back, gently rubbing his temples. Many things needed reworking. The accounting system was different from what he was used to, so it was a good thing Ty would be arriving in a few weeks' time.

With Ty's knowledge of international accounting practices, Thane could really use him.

He needed someone who understood the system—someone he could trust. Still, he could tell that the expenses were high. And a few suspicious practices needed further investigation. The due diligence paperwork MIA had sent to him in the US didn't support what he saw now. Could someone have intentionally misrepresented the state of the company to the partners? Running his fingers through his hair, Thane tried not to fuel his aggravation with negative thoughts. He hoped this trip wouldn't turn out to have been a waste—not when he had something as important as his career riding on it.

A picture sticking out of a pocket in his briefcase caught his eye. Pulling it out, he frowned. *Arlene?* He hadn't realized her photo was hidden in his briefcase. No doubt she'd put it there. Was it before or after she decided she didn't love him enough to stay with him? *Or* respect him enough to tell him she'd found someone else.

He stared at her bikini-clad image—the woman he'd once loved. The picture had been taken on their last vacation to Hawaii eighteen months ago. His heart hardened in anger. Even now, thoughts of her betrayal left a bitter taste in his mouth. He'd even introduced her to his parents—the first girl-friend he ever took home. He'd planned on marrying her and had taken it for granted that she wanted to marry him, too.

Shoving those thoughts out of his mind, he considered keeping the photo as a reminder of why he'd sworn off women, why he was absolutely not allowing any woman into his heart again. Hell, he wouldn't let a woman into his life. Period. He was done being vulnerable. His mother thought he'd get over it in time, but he didn't intend to. Deciding he didn't need a reminder, he tossed the picture into the trash.

He needed a drink and a long, cold shower then he'd work into the night. Time to return to the hotel, he thought, and made a mental note to look for an apartment. Staying at a hotel could get expensive even with the more than favorable exchange rate.

৫৩৫

Naaki Tabika woke early. She even had time to take a shower before her alarm went off. The countdown was finally over. She was about to get a foot in the door of her dream agency—Media Image Advertising. Excitement shimmied in her belly as she put on a touch of make-up. Then she slipped on the soft-peach blouse she'd picked out last night before heading to bed. Her suit was made of a colorful batik fabric—one of many such suits she owned. If she wanted to be taken as a professional, it was important to dress the part.

Dressed, she headed to the dining room for breakfast. While the pot of lemon grass tea brewed, she flipped through the *Daily Graphic*, circling some mildly interesting job prospects, none of which compared with MIA, but she needed to fulfill the internship requirement of her Chartered Marketing Certification course. If she didn't get into MIA—

The thought didn't fully materialize, as a news item caught her attention.

"In the final stage of the Media Image Advertising's makeover, Thane Aleksander, the International Account Director of US advertising firm, Black & Black, will be arriving in Accra..." she read the article aloud, noticing the spelling of the man's last name.

It was almost two years ago that the first news item about corruption at MIA had hit the newsstands. MIA, the acronym that used to elicit admiration and pride was now laughingly referred to as "Missing In Action" or worse. Granted, the General Manager had embezzled client funds and housed his mistress in a company-paid apartment, among other things. Negative relations between him and his staff had caused several of them to quit. Eventually, the agency's directors had come together and forced him to resign. They'd hired an acting managing director, while attempting to build a new management team.

Despite this, Naaki still held a great deal of admiration for the company, its history. Judging from the very positive outlook of the article in the papers today, MIA was well on its way to becoming the top agency again, and she wanted to be part of the process.

Heart pounding, she brought the large mug of steaming lemongrass tea to her mouth and took a sip, as if it would calm her mounting excitement. Her interview was in a few hours, and the thought of it filled her with a raging mix of exhilaration and nervousness.

Her cell phone rang. She answered it without checking the display since her mother always called to wish her luck whenever Naaki had a big day.

"Hi, mum." A smile tugged at the corner of her lips.

"Hello," her mother's gentle voice said. "How are you feeling?"

*Nervous.* "Excited."

"Good. You've done your homework, and I know you'll do well in the interview."

Naaki smiled again, although in her mind, she kept wondering what would happen if they picked someone else, someone better than her. For one, it would mean starting job hunting anew, which in turn meant a delay in her internship and her attainment of the esteemed title of Chartered Marketer—a title that would open many doors for her professionally.

Last year had been her first attempt at doing her compulsory internship towards her certification, although at the time she'd just wanted to get it over with. Then MIA had announced, after a three-year hiatus, that they'd be taking one intern this year. Since then, she'd spent her job hunting time researching MIA.

Working there had been her desire for a long time. Well...in the days when working there had been so prestigious that you practically had to know or be someone to get hired. All her career plans began with her at MIA. To think she might actually get in now rather than in five years' time! *If* she got in.

She sighed. "With the change of management, who knows how stringent the hiring criteria has become?"

Her mother gave a soft chuckle. "If they fail to see what an asset you'd be to their company, it will be their loss and some other company's gain."

Except, Naaki thought, there were no other interviews. She hadn't applied anywhere else—perhaps, in hindsight, not the wisest move. Well, today would determine the extent of her genius...or idiocy.

She couldn't bring herself to tell her mother what a major setback a rejection would be, so she said, "I know."

"Well, good luck, although you don't need it."

Warmth flowed into Naaki's heart. Her mother's confidence in her always boosted her morale. "Thanks, mum."

Returning to her breakfast after the call, she finished reading the newspaper article. Her three-month internship would be taking place smack in the middle of all the upcoming changes at MIA. She couldn't have planned it better.

*Thane Aleksander*. The name popped into her mind and she was surprised to discover she liked the sound of it. She knew of Black & Black from a few articles she'd read online. The agency was one of the most respected in America. With their rapid expansion into Europe and Asia, they had begun making waves in the industry worldwide. And according to the paper, Thane Aleksander had been at the forefront of that strategic expansion.

His coming to Ghana would no doubt be a big boost for MIA's damaged reputation, not to mention the country's advertising industry as a whole. Still, the thought of him filled her with a slight sense of...well...concern. What if he was just some hotshot with nothing but grand ideas, swooping in and tossing about words like "change" and "improvement"? She'd seen it happen many times before and not just in business. Americans slapped "expert" onto their titles and tried to force their western values on the local people regardless of the styles or cultures of the countries those people were in.

Naaki just hoped *Aleksander* made an effort to understand the local customs rather than simply imposing his company's policies on MIA. By the time she got into her car, she felt bold and confident—well, maybe just a tad nervous, judging from the rate of her heartbeat. Hopefully, Aleksander was impressed with her résumé.

"Only one way to find out," she muttered and started the car.

က္သာင

Thane pondered the work that would have to be done at MIA. The current clientele was too small to support a twenty-five-person workforce. They needed more clients, but in the meantime, though he didn't like it, they might have to lay people off. He tried not to get emotional about layoffs, but he hadn't thought it would be necessary here.

Now, he realized MIA needed a makeover. So far the agency was running a charity organization. They had to weed out some current personal and bring in a few key people who could move the agency forward.

*Speaking of new personnel.* He sighed and rubbed the back of his neck. Five candidates would be coming in to interview for a marketing internship today. MIA had to be careful whom they selected. They couldn't afford to waste time and money training people they wouldn't want to employ permanently.

He glanced at his watch. Damn, as much as he wanted to sit in on the interviews, he needed to go convince an angry client not to make good on their threat to drop the agency. If MIA lost any clients, Black & Black would lose interest in the merger, which could affect his chances of making partner any time soon.

As he headed for the door, he grabbed the banana that had been part of his official '*Akwaaba*' gift basket. He'd missed breakfast, so the fruit was very welcome. Trying to ignore the receptionist who apparently worshipped the ground he walked on, he gritted his teeth and kept walking, certain that her attitude would begin to irritate him soon.

He pulled his car key out of his pocket. It slipped through his fingers and he swore. As

18

he bent over to pick them up, the banana peel fell beside the keys. Muttering another curse, he impatiently tossed it aside, aiming for a large garbage can.

Then he noticed her...suit. A business suit for all intents and purposes except it was very colorful—made out of some tie-dyed-looking fabric. Against her dark skin, the effect was arresting. He stared.

In corporate America her clothes would probably not go down too well. Even students in business school were specifically advised to keep their attire to the traditional black or navy-blue suit. But somehow in Ghana, everything seemed more...vibrant and alive.

She wore her hair pulled back and walked with precise steps, clutching a manila folder. The combination of the woman, her suit, and her composure were...perfect.

Fashionable shades concealed her eyes but accentuated the soft curves of her cheekbones and her button nose. For a moment, he envisioned her black hair cascading down her shoulders, bouncing around her oval face as she made her way toward him. In fact, he wouldn't have minded helping her undo the bun.

He shook off the image. This was, he assumed, one of his co-workers. Even if he didn't have a "no dating" policy, he certainly didn't get frisky with co-workers. Arlene had taught him that. Thane stood up. Wait a minute, had he just described the woman approaching as perfect? As he walked toward her, he wondered if she'd noticed him at all, but when she passed without even an acknowledging nod, he assumed not.

Then he heard her voice.

"Excuse me, sir."

His heart did what felt suspiciously like a flip. *What the—*

She'd spoken in the most musical voice he'd ever heard. He turned to face her.

"I don't know where you come from, but I would think throwing a banana peel at someone without apologizing would be considered rude, especially when that person is your elder."

"What—" Thane glanced over at where the banana peel had fallen and noticed, only then, there was a man sitting a few feet from the trash can. Who the hell was he and why was he sitting there?

"A man is a whole lot more than a business suit," the mystery woman said, disapproval lacing her words, although what struck him more was the charming accent. There was something proper about the way she spoke, not prissy like the British. More...*exotic*. "And swearing like that...how would it look to a client?"

She left him standing there, staring after her. Had she just called him rude? Thane was usually unfazed by what people thought of him or what names they chose to call him. Yet having this beautiful stranger call him rude, elicited feelings strangely close to hurt. How could he be so affected by her words? Or was it rather the disappointment in her voice that struck a chord? He went to pick up the banana peel and dropped it in the trash where it should have landed in the first place. He apologized to the man who seemed good-natured about it.

Thane didn't look forward to meeting Ms. Perfect—officially, that is. No doubt she was the finance manager he hadn't yet met. Except, from everything he'd heard, his expectations were of someone older. Then a thought occurred to him that sent a discomforting chill down his spine. What if she wasn't just a colleague? *How would this look to a client*, she'd said. Great! Second day on the job and a client thought he was rude. *Way to go, Aleksander*. He could already see her contemplating ways of dropping MIA; although a nagging, uncharacteristic thought remained on his mind. Was a client considered a co-worker?

"Aw hell," he muttered. This was quickly looking unlike his usual business trips in more ways than one.

# CHAPTER 2

The meeting had been successful, but a great deal of work needed to be done. MIA had one very dissatisfied client who was unhappy with both agency relations and the quality of creative work produced over the past year. It seemed the only reason they still kept MIA was the history between the two companies, coupled with certain stipulations in their contract, and the latter was up for negotiation in a couple months. The client needed a reason to stay or they'd call for other proposals.

Back in his office, Thane momentarily pushed aside thoughts of the meeting to concentrate on the interviews. He was ready for the fourth applicant. The first three had been good but not impressive, which bothered him, considering he had hopes of finding someone who could join the team on a permanent basis. Sitting back, he picked up the next résumé, noticing the crisp cream-white paper. In addition to great references and a solid educational background, this applicant was getting a Chartered Marketing Certification, which he understood was the marketing equivalent of a CPA. The agency could use someone with these credentials. He scanned the document and made a few notes, then buzzed the office secretary to send in the candidate.

It was time to find out if the person matched the résumé.

When she walked in, Thane did a double-take. The pen he'd been twirling between his fingers slipped, clattering noisily on the desk. His attempt to catch it only caused it to bounce and fall off the edge of the desk, making his effort seem like fumbling. Biting back an expletive, he stooped to pick it up.

It was uncharacteristic of him to be taken aback by the presence of another, but then it wasn't every day he had to interview someone who'd called him rude just hours earlier. Somehow he'd have preferred it if she were a client. *They* could always be smooth-talked.

Having recovered from the initial shock, he straightened up and extended his hand, addressing her in his most business-like tone. "Thane Aleksander." He referred to her name on the résumé. "Naaki Tabika?"

"Yes," she replied, taking his hand.

"Did I get it right?" he asked. "I'm still learning how to pronounce the local names."

"Yes, you did." She sounded surprised.

Excellent. He could use the upper hand in whatever form it took.

She had a good grip, but her eyes betrayed a hint of worry. Thane held her hand longer than strictly necessary as he fought an involuntary pang of concern at her uneasiness. Yet, all the while, she looked him straight in the eye just as she'd done earlier, as if determined not to be intimidated. He motioned for her to sit and took his seat at the desk.

She sat like a beauty queen—graceful legs crossed at her ankles and hands on her lap one on top of the other—regarding him with her doe eyes. Bambi had nothing on her. Reviewing her résumé, he noted some pieces of personal information. Middle Initial: F; Marital Status: Single; Age: twenty-four; Weight: sixty kilograms; about a hundred and thirty pounds, by his calculation. That seemed about right, he thought, as his eyes did a pleasure tour of her body, taking in the contours of her legs and her curvy hips, traveling up her slender waist to her breasts. *Bra size?* Shocked by his train of thought, he kicked himself mentally and forced his gaze back to eye-level.

"How are you today?" he asked, trying to lighten the mood.

"Fine," she answered cautiously, ending with a ghost of a smile.

"So...what does the middle initial F stand for?" *What?* How on earth did she manage to make him feel incompetent? He was supposed to be interviewing her, yet from his behavior so far it could have been the other way around.

"Faith," she said.

The word echoed in his head like a prophecy. Faith was exactly what he needed to have in MIA. Looking into her eyes, he wondered if that applied in a literal sense.

He decided to skip further introductory questions. Things were awkward enough as it was. No need to prolong the torture—and the temptation to guess her bra size...or imagine how well her breasts would fit into his hands.

"Assume you were in my position and one of your most valued clients had threatened to drop the agency because they're dissatisfied with the quality of work," he began. "What would you do to keep them?"

A frown crossed her face as she considered the question. "If you're talking about jobs that are currently in-house, I'd suggest an emergency review of the advertising brief and a brainstorming session...maybe get one or two fresh people to add to the mix, even if it's people from the client's team."

"What if they aren't current jobs?" His attention dropped to her dainty fingers with which she gesticulated while talking.

"We can't fix past mistakes, but we can make sure current and future projects sweep them off their feet," she stated confidently.

Thane nodded, wondering briefly what would sweep her off her feet.

"In the meantime," she went on, "we'd have to ensure that all interactions with them are smooth. Billing shouldn't be unnecessarily cumbersome, because money tends to complicate things."

He nodded. He knew about complications, and allowing his thoughts to veer to her attractive physical attributes would definitely complicate things.

"Okay." He scribbled some points on his notepad, noticing specifically how she kept saying, "we." *Team player.* "Anything else? Especially on billing?"

Her eyes narrowed in concentration. "I don't know what the current system is, but clients should be billed only for jobs they actually approve and sign. In other words, jobs they're happy with."

Thane met her gaze, glad to note she appeared relaxed now. "Isn't that risky? What if you spend executive time and resources and your client decides they don't like the job?"

Her lips curved into a slight smile as if she'd known that question was coming. "I assume we work closely with our clients, so they would have to sign off at every stage of the process. It is to our benefit to serve them well, and it is to their benefit to help us do it."

Thane nodded attentively.

"That way," she continued, "the agency covers itself, and the client is still liable to pay for any part of a project they approved even if it never gets used. Failing that, we could bank on social relations."

He frowned, barely catching and pulling himself out from the depths of her bottomless brown eyes. "Social relations?"

Now she gave him a full smile, which lit up her eyes. The effect was like a punch in the gut. Thane swallowed. With very little makeup, she still looked stunning, and her expressions allowed him to appreciate her exotic beauty.

"Like a gala to celebrate the relationship we have," she said. "In this culture, friendship always makes people think twice before making a move that could be negative for the other party."

The "in this culture" comment didn't go unnoticed. Even as an interviewee, she was determined to set him straight. She was obviously well-informed and her confidence shone through intelligent eyes.

He'd never really cared what people thought of him, yet as he listened to her talk about herself and her knowledge of the company, it mattered what she had to say. He wanted to know her mind or maybe he just wanted to hear her voice. He hadn't decided yet what it was about her voice that affected him. Just that it went from his ears to somewhere deeper, filling his insides with warmth. It made the fact that she'd called him rude irritate the hell out of him.

He reined in his wandering thoughts as he asked his next question. "If you were responsible for expanding the company's client base, how would you go about it?"

"Do I have a time frame?"

"Throw anything at me."

She shifted in her seat, and he could have sworn she looked uncomfortable. Had he said something wrong?

"Just give me the first idea that springs to mind," he encouraged.

"Testimonials and case studies," she said. "They are a good way of informing people about our clients and what we've done for them. Many agencies tag TV ads with their logos. We can adapt that strategy to include everything—billboards, posters and so on. It will show we acknowledge the responsibility that we owe to each client for putting any-thing out in their name."

He nodded, jotting down a few points he didn't want to forget. "So your idea is to demonstrate that we're not just an agency but more of a partner?"

"Exactly."

She was smiling again. It shouldn't have meant anything, but he found himself breathing easier.

He kept her for almost forty minutes trying to find a reason why she didn't fit the position. Unprofessional, yes, but a better excuse than the one he was trying to ignore. Finally, when no reason was forthcoming, he asked his last question, "How willing are you to poach clients from the competition?"

He watched her bite her lips and frown. She looked so adorable doing that, Thane had to fight the urge to smile.

"It depends," she finally replied. "If the client is unhappy with their current agency, and if I can serve them better, then yes."

He wondered how aggressive she'd be in business development. "Thank you, Ms. Tabika." He stood. "We'll be contacting you in a few business days."

"Thank you," she said, also standing.

As he walked her out of the door, he said, more out of curiosity than anything else, "One more question."

She turned to face him, standing so close he caught a whiff of her fresh autumn breeze scent. He had to take a step backwards to avoid leaning in. "What other companies did you apply to?"

"I only applied to MIA." She hesitated as though there was more, but didn't continue.

He quirked a brow. "You were job hunting and you applied to only one company? That was rather..." Not finding a better word he said, "...foolish, wasn't it?"

*Shit*! Thane couldn't believe he'd just said that. The shock in her eyes mirrored his own surprise at her calling him rude earlier, and to his shame it gratified him. Why was he behaving like a fifteen-year-old boy experiencing his first crush? Even at fifteen he hadn't had a crush this big, if ever. What was it about this woman?

She was about to say something when Mr. Boateng, coming toward them, interrupted. "Great. We're down to the last one."

Thane's attention shifted as he responded. "Yes, we are."

When he turned back to Naaki, she was walking away. He wanted to call her back and apologize for his comment. It was none of his business where else she'd applied or how many applications she'd made. His business was to assess whether she'd be a good fit for MIA. Lord only knew why he cared to the point of exhibiting juvenile behavior, though in his defense, he'd meant to say foolhardy. The "ish" just slipped in.

With regret, he watched her disappear round the corner.

The next candidate had a big task ahead of him if he intended to top Naaki Tabika's assertiveness and all the things about her that were so inexplicably attractive.

ᘒᘑᘒᘑ

Naaki's whole body shook as she stepped outside the building. Her eyes burned with the tears she fought to keep at bay. She didn't have to be a genius to know her chances of getting the internship were close to nil. If she'd believed going back and groveling would do any good, she'd be knocking down Thane Aleksander's office door and begging for mercy instead of standing outside MIA like a lost child, wondering how she'd allowed such an opportunity to slip through her fingers.

An hour later, after she got home, her pulse still raced erratically, despite every effort to think rationally about her options. The annoying out-of-breath feeling that accompanied nervousness was there, pell-mell. Off the top of her head, she'd made a list of other agencies she could apply to, then spreading out the last three days' *Daily Graphic* on her dining table, which doubled as a workspace, she circled a few other prospects. If she'd gotten an interview with MIA, someone else was bound to be interested in her. She only hoped it wasn't too late.

She swallowed down the sick feeling in her stomach. Of all the scenarios that had played through her mind in the past couple of weeks while preparing for the interview, this hadn't been one of them. Even when she finally tucked her pencil into the notepad, satisfied for now with the list she'd developed, her mind refused to fully accept that MIA was a lost cause.

She realized she might have to confront her feelings at some point, and maybe allow herself to shed the tears she so desperately tried not to.

If only she had someone to talk to. But whom? If she called her mother, she'd have to talk about the interview, and Naaki didn't want to have to lie. Since turning eighteen, her mother had become more of a confidante than a parent. Apart from the fact that she didn't like lying, Naaki definitely didn't like doing so to her mother. For the same reason, her best friend, Patricia Owusu, was also not an option.

She thought about calling Gyamfi. *No way.* Breaking up with him was the best decision she'd ever made. Even though there were times she'd wondered whether theirs had been true love, it had still surprised her when he'd given her an ultimatum—him or a career. It had hurt to discover he thought her goals and dreams were secondary to his.

The only problem with the break up was that their families were friends. His mother still hoped she'd come to her senses and accept her son's offer of marriage and family. Only, Gyamfi's proposal had come with a price tag she couldn't afford. Why was it so hard for them to believe she wanted to be a career woman? Of course, she wanted a family too. Were family and career mutually exclusive?

She bit her lip uncertainly, wishing for some lemongrass tea. Alas, there was none left in the house after this morning's break-fast. It was too dark in the backyard to go and cut some fresh leaves—even with her flashlight. She'd have to remember to change the bulb tomorrow. She felt an urge to bite her nails; a bad teenage habit she'd weaned herself from a long time ago. She hadn't felt the need in ages, but she was anxious. And for good reason.

Normally she didn't let things get to her, but with the combination of her branding Mr. Aleksander as rude and him calling her fool-ish, she had a lot to worry about. If she didn't do her internship now, it would delay her studies and increase her expenses. She couldn't afford either. Why hadn't she just ignored the obvious disregard for an elderly person's rights just this one time?

She sighed. Maybe Gyamfi was right. Perhaps she was deluding herself that she had something unique to offer to the business world. The temptation to call him became stronger. With his take-charge attitude he'd be here promptly, ready to comfort and "take care" of her. But after she'd told him what had happened he'd probably call her foolish, too.

As the owner of a successful brokerage firm, Gyamfi's sense of self-importance was in many ways well-earned. However, it left no room for anyone else. Not even for her—supposedly the most important person in his life. No. There had to be something else she could do to calm her nerves.

*Cook.* Yes, she would cook. She decided on yams, since she had some vegetable stew in the fridge. Taking out a tuber, she cut what she needed and began working on it.

Though the task demanded some of her attention, it wasn't enough to stop her mind from wandering back to today's events and Thane Aleksander. She'd been to many interviews, but none had been quite as easygoing. That is, if she discounted the awkwardness of sitting in front of him, while wondering whether he'd bring up their earlier encounter. The questions he'd asked had been simple. More than that, he'd seemed genuinely interested in what she could contribute to the agency, which sadly endeared him to her.

As she prepared supper—forget worrying about how she did in the interview—she was thinking about his eyes; a gorgeous gray, with fascinating flecks of gold. She hadn't seen that before. In Ghana, as she suspected was the case in most of Africa, there were just different shades of brown. Staring into his eyes, she'd had a sensation of swimming in the ocean at sunset when the water looked gray rather than blue. His thin lips, which lent beauty to simple spoken words, were a bubblegum pink that made her wonder what they tasted like. Embarrassed at her train of thought, she had to remind herself that she was alone and could indulge in whatever thoughts she pleased. Including what those bubblegum lips tasted like.

Besides, chances were she wasn't going to see him again, so what was the harm?

He had to be the most handsome man she'd ever met. It wasn't often that she described a man as handsome. For her, the word meant something more than just good-looking. In fact, she wasn't certain she could describe in words what a handsome man was, but she'd always believed she'd know one when she met him. And Thane, with his chiseled nose and angular features, definitely was handsome.

Her heartbeat assumed a riotous tempo. He'd made her so aware of herself, without eliciting the feeling that her femininity was under threat, as she often experienced around other men who were so proudly male.

Peeling the last piece of yam, she remembered his last words to her and her heart tightened. She didn't know why it had hurt, but it did. Almost as much as the day Gyamfi had asked her to choose between him and her "silly dreams." She'd known it was risky applying to only one place, but as she'd dug deeper into the top agencies, she became so consumed with MIA that, eventually, there'd been no time or desire to apply anywhere else.

How was she to know that the same man she'd insulted earlier in the day would have her fate in his hands? He would probably pass her up for somebody else—maybe the only guy in the group. Men had a way of sticking together.

It was just her luck that he should arrive a week earlier than the papers announced, just to make her life difficult. She definitely didn't like the rude and presumptuous Thane Aleksander.

So why did she remember the warmth of his hand when he shook hers? Why did his voice make her heart feel like dancing? Why was she thinking about him at all?

❧✦❧

"My recommendations are Paul Opoku and Naaki Tabika," Mr. Boateng said. "They both excelled in the orientation exercises and exhibited a sense of initiative. They'd done their research and asked very pertinent questions."

Thane had asked Mr. Boateng into his office to discuss the internship candidates. He listened with keen interest as the other man spoke. He'd also narrowed the choice down to Naaki and Paul. Reviewing both their résumés, he asked, "Did either of them come across as a stronger candidate?"

Mr. Boateng shook his head with a sigh. "I can't really say that. Ghanaian women tend to be gentle in nature and less aggressive, and sometimes it's not a good thing, especially for an agency trying to win new business." He cleared his throat and continued, "However, Naaki may not necessarily be the shy type. Before the orientation began, I observed them for a little while. I noticed she made an effort to talk to everyone."

Thane imagined her lecturing them on proper interviewing etiquette. The thought made him smile. For someone so petite she was daring—he had to hand it to her. But it was more than her brazen attitude that he liked. There was something else—a genuineness about her—that caught his attention.

"On the other hand, Paul is unquestionably bold albeit with a bit of a leader complex," Mr. Boateng continued.

"Yes, I sensed that, too, but with effective guidance and training he could be molded into a great team member," Thane said. At least he wouldn't feel guilty if they ended up choosing Paul. He decided to share some of his plans with Mr. Boateng. "I've been considering the possibility of extending the attachment to full employment once the three months are up."

"It's an excellent idea. We need new blood in the agency. Some of the old staff have grown complacent." With that, Mr. Boateng stood. "Frankly, I'd be happy with either of the two. It's unfortunate we can't take them both."

Thane could certainly understand the sentiment. Once trained, both candidates could bring a lot to the agency.

"Well, the ball is in your court," Mr. Boateng said. "Although, considering your idea of permanent employment, a female will help the gender balance of the agency."

Again, Thane found himself smiling, wondering what Naaki would say to that comment. He'd spent so little time with her, yet he felt he'd seen enough to know she wouldn't like to be hired just to even out the gender balance. "Thank you, Mr. Boateng."

"You're welcome." At the door Mr. Boateng turned. "I'm meeting with the marketing manager of Asante Motors for drinks. My inside source says they'll be looking for an agency soon. It might be a good opportunity to introduce you, if you aren't busy."

"I'm not." Thane welcomed the opportunity for networking. An informal meeting would provide an excellent opening to study this potential client. He'd sealed many deals over drinks, including some that weren't even on the table yet. "Give me a couple of minutes to pack up."

Hopefully drinks with a potential client would drive away the memory of Naaki and her exquisite brown eyes.

# CHAPTER 3

"Concentrate on the next five days," Naaki muttered to herself. She'd stopped counting how many times she'd needed to say something along those lines to calm her nerves, which seemed unusually raw since the interview.

A full week had passed and she hadn't heard anything from MIA. No doubt Thane Aleksander had decided to pass her up. She wished his name would stop popping into her thoughts. She hated the way her heart somersaulted when she thought about him—even when she was telling herself she didn't like him. Truth be told, he stirred up feelings she'd never experienced before. The man was gorgeous. And that assessment applied to everything about him, from his tall, masculine frame to the details of his gray eyes, and the warmth of his hands when he had held hers. His smile...

She'd get over it, she told herself. After all, she'd never see him again. If the final selection depended on him, as she expected it did, then she had probably been out of the running before the interview.

Good thing she'd signed up last month to be a hostess at the Pan African conference being held at La Paulanda Hotel. At the time, she'd hoped to get more data for her final written report for her certification. Now, it also provided an avenue for putting Plan B into motion. There would be important dignitaries from all over Africa and the Diaspora attending; she was bound to meet some prospective employers. If nothing else, it would be a captivating showcase of culture and color.

And if she got to stay at a posh hotel free of charge for five days, it was okay with her.

She eased her old VW Beetle into an empty spot in the guest parking lot. Sitting beside a Mercedes and a brand new Q7, the Volkswagen looked out of place, but she didn't care. Even though she loved her car, she had no problem parting with it for five days during which time she could pretend to be a VIP.

She straightened out her skirt and wheeled her two pieces of luggage to the hotel's main entrance where a concierge quickly came to her aid. When she stepped into the plush lobby, thoughts of Thane Aleksander took a momentary back seat as the idea of being part of such a historic event brought on a surge of excitement.

ᕫᗧᕫ

Thane called his mother as soon as he returned from the gym downstairs. He'd been in Ghana a week, and knowing Celeste Aleksander, she'd be waiting for his call. Not surprisingly, she was baking. One of the neighbors had a baby a few days ago, she explained. Thane smiled. His mother needed no excuse to bake. Between cooking and baking, it was a wonder she'd remained as slender as she was when she had been a model at age twenty-one—a career she'd happily given up when she met Thane's father.

"Hi, mom," he said, his voice full of affection.

"Thane." She sounded as if she'd been expecting to hear his voice. "How are you doing? How was your flight?"

"I'm fine, and the flight was uneventful, as it should be."

"How's Africa? Ghana, is it?"

"Beautiful," he said, an image of Naaki unequivocally forming before his mind's eye. "Very beautiful."

"Glad you like it, honey," his mother said. "Will you be back by Thanksgiving?"

"I don't know. I'm supposed to babysit this project for six months unless it takes off smoothly before then."

She made a sound to express her disappointment. "Well, try to make it. The Patricks have an unmarried granddaughter two years your junior."

"I don't have time for a relationship right now."

"Honey, you need to see new people. Even if it's on the rebound. It isn't healthy at all, the way you're carrying on as if you never intend to date again."

He'd never been the type to start any relationship with a short-term view, although after Arlene he'd only managed two short-lived relationships, both of which ended up being purely physical. That was when he decided he was done with relationships altogether.

"Mother." He called her that when she was getting under his skin. Especially because she hated it. "I only called to tell you I got here in one piece, not to be grilled about my love life."

"Oh, Thane, you know I only want you to be happy. It was terrible to see you heartbroken after Arlene ran off with that—what's-his-name?"

*Brad Van Dusen.* It wasn't just the fact that she left him for that idiot. He'd had to find out from the front page of a newspaper—along with the rest of America. "Water under the bridge," he said, quickly blocking out the memory. "I have to go."

"Okay, honey. Call again soon."

"Will do, Mom."

After a shower he felt refreshed and settled down to do some work. He needed to get a lot done if he wanted to be prepared for Monday's meetings. He'd seen a few notices downstairs about a conference to be held over the next few days, and he didn't know how distracting it would be. *Better get the bulk of the job done tonight.*

He also needed to call Steven Black to finalize their negotiation strategy. The initial
plan had been to invest resources into MIA
and set up a partnership, allowing the local
agency to keep a separate identity by merg-
ing theirs and Black & Black's company
rules and culture. That was before Black &
Black landed their latest client, an international hotel group, boosting the agency's
portfolio. Two days before Thane left the
US, Steve and his brother, Leo, the partners
at Black & Black, had changed their minds
about the terms of the negotiations.

On the surface the present deal would still
benefit MIA, but it wasn't as good as the initial plan. Actually, Thane could easily justify
the change with the fact that MIA's true state
of affairs had been misrepresented. Still, he
didn't like it. He had a gut feeling he didn't
have all the facts. There was always someone
holding on to potentially vital information in
the hopes of using it as a trump card. He just
had to make sure he didn't end up as a pawn
in whatever game was going on. Assuming,
of course, that there was a game.

He felt tired even though he hadn't been
working more than an hour. Had to be the
humidity. After one week, he still wasn't

used to it. Usually he had more energy than this.

The phone in his suite rang. He suspected it was the front desk, calling to find out if he wanted room service or whatever else they could lavish on him.

"Hello," he answered welcoming the interruption, but as he listened he changed his mind about being relieved. The manager informed him about a reservation oversight—the conference was over-booked, and they hoped Thane wouldn't mind giving up the adjoining room to a conference delegate. He had every intention of saying no. He'd booked that extra space for meetings and was currently working there, but the guy was persistent.

Finally, reluctantly, he gave in. It was only for a few days. Besides, he was thinking of moving into an apartment where he'd have all the space he needed. The manager all but promised Thane his first-born child, but that didn't make Thane any happier about giving up his "office." However, as the man explained, the person was conference staff and needed to be at this hotel.

He hung up before realizing he hadn't asked when the person would be arriving, but he planned half an hour to find a new place for his papers in his suite. Five minutes later, he heard a knock.

Thane frowned. He hadn't ordered anything so it couldn't be room service. He opened the door only slightly to see the manager's apologetic face.

"Mr. Aleksander, thank you for your kindness. It will not go unnoticed by management."

"They're already here?"

"Yes, sir. Unfortunately, we only noticed the problem when she arrived."

*She*? Thane frowned. Nobody said anything about a she, he thought irritably. He didn't know why it bothered him. It wasn't as if they were asking him to *share* the room.

"We can have her wait in the lounge if you need time," the man said, then added uncertainly as if wondering whether it was appropriate. "It's just that she looks tired."

"No, I'll move my papers right away." He gave a smile that had to look as fake as it felt.

The cart bearing the luggage arrived first and Thane couldn't help noticing there were only two medium-sized pieces. Most women he knew, his mother included, would need a lot more than two suitcases for a five-day conference. The owner of the bags followed the bellboy in, and for a moment, Thane had to put a firm clamp on his tongue to stop himself from cursing. Somebody had to be playing with his luck, because this evening sure as hell wasn't going his way.

Her eyes flared with obvious surprise, which she quickly masked. At least he wasn't the only one taken unawares. Thane didn't attempt to hide his displeasure. Because a part of him *was* happy to see her, and he couldn't have that.

After another round of profuse gratitude the manager, who didn't seem to notice the tense atmosphere between the two guests, left the room.

She did look tired, Thane observed after he'd shelved the idea of taking the room back. He studied her for a moment. Just like before, her hair was tied back, but instead of the business suit, she wore a more casual skirt and short-sleeved jacket. The open jacket revealed a cream-colored tank top that showed a hint of cleavage, but it was what he couldn't see that intrigued him. Though the fabric looked soft, he couldn't see her nipples. He fought the desire to guess how many strokes of his thumb would make them bead up, begging to be released at his touch.

*Whoa, get a grip, Aleksander.* Not for the first time, he forced himself to maintain his gaze at eye level. The dark brown—almost black—eyes, threatened to cripple his senses. She was petite—not small—with skin the color of pure honey and lips that begged to be kissed. Thane shook himself mentally.

As if he didn't have more than enough reasons why he shouldn't think of her along those lines. She met his gaze without speaking. *Now what?* Funny, he'd never had to wonder what to say to a woman.

"Thanks for the room," she said.

Thane's voice caught as he tried to respond. He cleared his throat. "No biggie." He managed a shrug as if he didn't care. But, oh, did he care.

She began to move her luggage, and the sight of her trying to lift the large suitcases triggered a rush of old-fashioned masculine feelings of chivalry. "Let me."

က်ာ

"I can—" Naaki started to protest, but her words died away when their eyes met. She caught a whiff of his aftershave. Something subtle, but it sent her heart into palpitations. Calm down, she told herself, but it was pointless. His hand brushed hers as he took hold of the suitcase, sending a shiver up her spine. Under his gaze, there was no relaxing. The only smart thing to do was allow him to take charge of the luggage.

She stepped back and watched him lift the first one as though it weighed next to nothing. He placed it close to the wardrobe. It was a good location. She wouldn't have to do much to-and-fro as she unpacked, for which she was grateful. Fatigue had begun to set in.

Leaving the second case next to the first, Thane pinned her with his gray eyes, his gaze hard and impenetrable. His hands rose to rest on his lean hips. Only then did she notice how close to the door the wardrobe was. *Oh my God, he's going to throw me out!*

He couldn't do that, could he? She wouldn't put it past him. She squared her shoulders, as righteous anger surfaced. Despite her throbbing heartbeat, she wasn't going to be intimidated. He might have the power to deny her the internship, but she had as much right to be here, even if he was a paying guest and she wasn't. Besides he'd get a refund for the time she was staying. What did he need two rooms for, anyway?

"I'll be out of here in ten minutes," he said finally.

Naaki barely managed to keep her jaw from dropping as he walked past her to the table where he started to clear his stuff. He was letting her stay? Why? He obviously didn't seem happy about it. Perhaps he'd had no choice. What had the manager told him? Her heart sank. This had to be a sign—a bad one. She'd been praying all week for some act of providence to get her the job at MIA even after her ill-advised remarks. Now here she was encroaching on his space. She could forget about providence.

In spite of that, she couldn't help feeling grateful to him for giving up the room. At least Plan B was still on course.

As promised, Thane cleared out his laptop and documents in ten minutes. Naaki breathed a sigh of relief. Taking off her coat, she sank into the sofa that stood beside the bed. Unexpected exhaustion began to settle on her like a heavy cloud. After arguing with the receptionist and ranting about the overbooking, she wanted to take a shower to cool off and find something to eat. As it was, she'd waited too long to fill her stomach. She took a deep breath and exhaled through her mouth. Just then, her phone rang. It was Pat.

"Hi."

"Have they found you a room yet?"

"Yes." Naaki slipped off her shoes and curled her legs beneath her. "One guest had an extra room he was willing to give up for a few days."

"An extra room? Is he with his family?"

"I don't think so. At least he's not wearing a ring, although, these days, that doesn't mean much."

"You noticed he isn't wearing a ring?"

Naaki scowled. She'd walked straight into that one. "I didn't go out of my way to look. He carried my suitcases." Bullied them out of her hands was probably a better expression.

Pat's excited gasp didn't help matters. "He gave you his room *and* carried your luggage? Let me know when he invites you for dinner."

"Trust me, that's not going to happen." He was probably rethinking his decision to give up the room.

Pat made a sound. "Well, as long as you got a room. I'm shocked the hotel would make such an error, though."

"I know. It gives them a bad name, and I told them so."

"Oh, Naaki, you didn't." Pat laughed. "One day you're going to get in trouble for that mouth of yours."

Sharing her unsolicited opinion had already gotten her in trouble, but Naaki didn't think Pat needed to know that yet. "I was merely stating the obvious."

"I wish I were in Accra this week. We could have done a sleepover at the hotel."

Naaki sighed. A sleepover would have been fun, but it was out of the question since Pat was in Cape Coast, taking care of her sick mother, who didn't trust modern medicine. "When are you returning?"

Pat sighed. "Not before Sunday, unfortunately. After all mum's been through, she's still bull-headed about taking her medication. Can you believe it?" She heaved a melodramatic sigh. "Her current prescription finishes on Friday and she has a checkup on Saturday."

Naaki smiled. "She'll get better soon, don't worry."

"Yes, well, if she has enough energy to fight with me about the medicine, she has to be getting better. Speaking of which, it's time for another struggle."

"Remind her you're not ready to say goodbye to her."

"What haven't I told her? I've even threatened to remain single and never have babies, since she's been pestering me about grandchildren again."

Naaki chuckled. She couldn't imagine that going well with Pat's mother who was very anxious to see her only daughter settle down and have children. "Anyway, say hello to her for me."

"I will," Pat said. "And get something to eat. You know what happens when you don't eat."

Yes, she knew. "Food is the next item on my list, don't worry."

"Good girl."

Naaki rolled her eyes. "Talk to you to-morrow?"

"Yes, bye."

Disconnecting, she smiled, shaking her head as she imagined the fight Pat was un-doubtedly going to have with her mother. A light tapping sound made her sit up with a frown. Was that a knock? It sounded like it came from the adjoining door. A wave of unwelcome excitement stole into her. She chided herself. What would he be doing knocking on the door? *Really.* In his book she was a nuisance. Period. She leaned back in the chair, but the soft knock came again. No, she wasn't imagining it, she decided, and went over to open it.

The sight of him made her heart flutter and she swallowed, caught off guard by just how heart-stoppingly handsome he was. Had he been that good-looking before or had he become—if it were possible—even more so? The t-shirt hugging his torso and well-toned arms made her wonder how often he worked out. Wearing it with corduroy trousers, he oozed a maleness that was almost intoxicating—a maleness that made her feel incredibly female.

"Hi." She couldn't tear her eyes away even as she tried to remind herself that she didn't like him.

"I ordered room service. It looks like I got too much for one person," he explained, sounding apologetic. "Would you consider having dinner with me?"

Naaki shook her head. She had to be dreaming, imagining that her gorgeous would-have-been boss—had it not been for her unintelligent declaration of his lack of manners—was asking her to have a meal with him.

"That's kind of you, but the conference is providing my meals."

"I believe they had dinner earlier," he said.

Her gaze darted to the food cart behind him. The aroma wafting to her nostrils made her stomach rumble in anticipation. She froze for a moment, but he didn't seem to notice.

"What do you say?"

"I, uh..."

"They promised it was good, and I have a bottle of champagne."

"I—I don't drink with strangers," she responded, but her mind was thinking, *Are we celebrating something?*

"But we aren't strangers, Naaki Tabika." He flashed a female-weakening smile that intensified the gray of his eyes. "Sure we got off to a bad start, but I know you're twenty-four, five-six tall, and studying to earn your professional membership with the Chartered

Institute of Marketing. *I* am thirty-two and in Ghana on business. Plus we both have a vested interest in MIA."

He stepped back and opened the door further.

"Well..." she tried to think of reasons why she shouldn't. Like the way she felt winded when he looked into her eyes. She could suffocate in his presence. But she was hungry, and he was right about the conference dinner. "I suppose the chef won't be too pleased if the food went to waste."

He smiled. "It's settled then."

It was a good thing she didn't have it in mind to protest further, because the smile robbed her of words. She had no other choice than to accept the invitation.

The suite was significantly larger than hers, and, perhaps because of his presence, seemed more imposing, more masculine. A short distance behind him she noticed the corner of a large well-laid bed through an open door. Frowning at the out of character impulse to crawl under the sheets, she diverted her attention to the beautiful set of comfortable-looking furniture that beckoned her to sit. She sank onto one facing the TV, which was muted on CNN news. She shifted her focus from the silent images and watched as he set the food out on the coffee table.

As they ate, they talked about nothing in particular, but no other conversation she could remember had made her feel so exhilarated. When he asked her to tell him about Ghana, she was only too happy to oblige. She must have spoken for five minutes straight, encouraged by the interest in his eyes.

"I hope you get a chance to see more of Accra at least."

He didn't comment on that. Instead, he said, "I have a question for you."

"Okay." Naaki sat up unable to believe how much she was enjoying herself. Where had the brashness gone? How come she could only think of how easily she could lose herself in his eyes? In this instance, they looked so sincere, her heart skipped beats just wondering what his question might be.

"At the interview, you mentioned that you might have ideas to help retain a major client. Can you elaborate on some of those ideas?"

"Well, first, you have to treat every interaction with the client as if the relationship depends on it. Also—" She paused, alarmed at how easily he had gotten her talking. This wasn't an interview. "Wait a minute, they are my ideas. If you used them it would be your word against mine."

"My word against yours?"

"In court," she clarified.

He chuckled and sat back, looking terribly amused. "You would sue me?"

"Of course," she replied, feeling aggravatingly embarrassed at the smile playing around the corners of his lips. "If—if I had to."

"Well, that takes care of the nagging debate of whether or not you're a softy." He leaned forward looking intently at her. "What if I gave you my word that your ideas wouldn't be used without your permission?"

There it was again, that out-of-breath sensation. She could feel his stare as strongly as if he'd touched her. "I..." Her voice trailed off, and she had to remind herself to breathe.

"Ok, tell you what." He grabbed a paper and pen, scribbled furiously for over a minute and then slid the paper to her. "Here's your assignment. Write a proposal—copyright it if you wish—and give me a call on Friday. Better still drop by to let me know how far you've gotten with it."

She swallowed. "Sure."

As she took the papers, his hands brushed over hers sending a cascade of shivers down her spine and up again. Her heart was beating so hard she wondered if he could hear it. *Better leave now.*

"It's getting late," she said, getting to her feet.

"Yeah, I need to get some work done."

"And I have to get up early for the conference." An awkward silence fell between them as a desire to be hugged by him filled her.

"Thank you for sharing dinner with me, Naaki."

"You're welcome." She smiled, unable to believe she didn't really want to go. "Thanks for inviting me."

She began to walk toward her room, wanting so badly to turn around and take another peek at those broad shoulders that looked as if they could hug away all her worries.

"Wait," he called out.

She breathed deeply and her heart gave a lurch as butterflies fluttered in her stomach. She was shocked by the realization that she wanted him to ask her to stay a little longer.

Obnoxious, rude, sexy, great company. Which one was he? She turned around.

"I may have left a few papers in the room. Just knock on the door if you come across anything that might be mine."

"I'll be on the lookout."

She tried to remind herself that she'd sworn to remain single until she knew—really knew—what she wanted with her own life. Another disastrous relationship with an alpha male on a power trip was definitely not what she needed. She had to concentrate on getting an internship and gaining her certified CIM membership.

With a final glance, she said, "Good night."

"G'night." Thane smiled, one thumb hooked in the waist of his pants and the other hand raised to wave her goodnight.

ॐ

The door shut as if in slow motion, leaving Thane to be swallowed by the ensuing silence. He remained standing, feeling rather disconcerted. Should he have shaken her hand? He'd wanted to, but didn't—not with the way his hormones had been running wild around her since day one. Touching her would only uncover one more thing he could find attractive.

He shook his head, amazed at how delightful dinner with her had been. They'd started off on the wrong foot and something in him desired strongly to change that. He couldn't remember a time when he'd felt so comfortable in the company of another. His mind settled on the way she ate, the movements of her delicate fingers, how she occasionally licked her lips. She had a healthy appetite and didn't seem obsessed about carbs and all the diet scares that had hit America lately. Something he instantly liked about her.

With Arlene, dinner had always been an arduous task of calling restaurants, investigating menus and ensuring they had low-fat and organic everything with meatless meat. She couldn't cook to save her life, and didn't like to eat in the same place more than twice in a month.

But with Naaki...a smile tugged at the corners of his lips as he thought about the way her eyes danced when she talked about Ghana. Obviously, she loved her country.

And *he* just loved to listen to her musical voice.

A vivid image of her telling him stories of her childhood while she lay in his arms materialized out of nowhere. He brought it to a screeching halt and reminded himself that he couldn't afford to let his guard down around her. What was happening to him? This girl was off limits for more reasons than one; plus, by her own admission, she thought he was rude. Even if he knew he was anything but, he had no business dwelling on things that could never be.

He called room service, and within minutes they came to pick up the cart.

The lonesomeness he felt was unexpected. He needed to work on his resolve when it came to Naaki, starting now. He drew in a deep breath, exhaling through his mouth and took out his laptop. He'd never been more reluctant to perform a task—especially when it had to do with work. However, work was the only thing that was going to save him from himself tonight.

# CHAPTER 4

It had been a long couple of days since Naaki had dinner with Thane. Aside from conference duties, she'd networked to secure both job and informational interviews. One delegate had specifically mentioned an internship opening in his company and asked for her résumé. All in all, she'd had a couple of productive days.

Conference packs for the day in her hand, she lingered in the front lobby chatting with delegates who stopped by on their way to their rooms. She politely turned down invitations for tea and made her way to the bookstore. After being there fifteen minutes without finding anything of interest, she acknowledged to herself that she was hovering.

It was almost seven o'clock—about the time Thane returned from work. A glimpse was all she wanted. The confidence he exuded even when he walked commanded attention. It must be part of what made him such a formidable success. She could learn a thing or two just by watching him. No harm done.

Okay, she finally conceded, hanging around just for a peek at him was silly. She wasn't a teenager, after all. Having convinced herself that her behavior was completely absurd, she settled on a magazine.

დდდ

Thane spotted her as soon as he entered the hotel lobby and paused for a moment. He'd thought about her today—a lot. How the conference was going, whether she'd started on the assignment...what color her suit would be. What *combination* of colors, he corrected, taking in the tie-dye fabric that constituted her outfit. A smile crept to his lips. He wasn't sure when exactly he'd decided to say, "Hi," but he found himself standing by her side as she paid for a *Readers' Digest*. There was no indication that she'd noticed him. Thane grabbed a copy of

*USA Today*—international edition—since he already got local papers in the office.

"Hi there." He injected an inflection in his tone, pretending he'd only just noticed her.

"Hi." She chanced him a glance before returning her attention to the salesperson then turned to leave.

"How's the conference going?" he asked just to keep her from running off while he paid for his paper.

"Quite well." She didn't elaborate but continued out of the small shop.

"Wait," Thane said, stepping back into the main lobby after her. She stopped. "My proposal. How's that going? Have you been able to start on it?"

"Why would you think I haven't started, Mr. Aleksander?" She regarded him with a defiant look that dared him to question her further.

How had he managed to put her on the defensive so quickly? His strategy had to change pronto. He turned on phase one of Plan B—the Thane Aleksander smile.

"I suppose that's the wrong way to ask if you needed any input from me." The smile and what seemed like an apology often worked like a charm. "Call me Thane."

She didn't react to the smile. Instead, she surveyed him awhile, as if trying to decide whether to trust him.

Phase two—the stare. He caught her gaze and held it. Not threateningly but firm enough to communicate that he meant business. He'd sealed many deals with the stare.

"Thank you for offering. I do have a few notes I'd like to check with you," she finally said, the defiance in her voice clearly toned down. "Mainly policy issues and background information."

Thane moved in for the kill. "I'm just about to have a bite. Care to join me? We can discuss it over dinner." Food seemed to have worked once. No harm in trying it again.

"Thank you, but I've already eaten. Besides, I'm working." She didn't seem apologetic. "Conference official," she added, pointing at the badge pinned to her breast— er, bodice. "I need to make sure everything is set for tomorrow's activities."

"Okay." Thane felt a tad concerned. The stare didn't seem to be getting him anywhere with her, but with another two-year contract

signed today he was in the mood to celebrate, so he tried again. "Then join me for a
drink afterwards. I'll be done with dinner."

"It could take a while."

"I'll wait." Now that he'd latched onto
the idea, he wasn't about to let go, even if he
had to drag her downstairs. That thought
brought very tempting images to mind. He
had to fight the urge to laugh when he imagined her telling him off for dragging a woman in public. He wondered if she'd kick and
scream. She probably would. He wanted to
spend time with her. He didn't exactly know
why, but at least he wanted her to *like* him.
Nothing wrong with that, right?

For a stretch of time she simply returned
his stare without responding. Thane main-
tained an unreadable expression, trying in
turn to read hers. Dammit, it wasn't supposed to be this hard trying to get a woman
to have a drink with him. It wasn't as if he'd
invited her to his room. Actually, *that* he'd
done—and quite successfully.

Hell! This woman was messing with his
head, and Thane began to worry that he'd set
himself up for a fall. For once the stare was
going to let him down.

Finally, her look softened and she gave what seemed like the slightest of nods—he wasn't even sure about it being a nod—then turned around and hesitated a fraction before continuing on her way. Hoping that was a "yes," because it wasn't a definite "no," Thane proceeded downstairs for dinner.

ⓒⓈⓒⓈ

It took an hour and a half to complete an impromptu meeting and get all the conference material set up for tomorrow. Then she stopped by the business center for fifteen minutes to check emails, send out her résumé to those who'd requested it and Google a few people she wanted to talk to tomorrow. She spent five more minutes in the restroom touching up her makeup before heading downstairs. Would he still be there?

Just as she was about to descend the stairs, she saw him zip up his laptop case and stand. She stopped abruptly. His face was drawn into a stiff, unreadable mask. That couldn't be his happy face. When he jerked the case off the table, she decided facing him would be tantamount to suicide. Especially when he looked like he could spew out words worse than "foolish" in one breath. Particularly not when the look was meant for her. Assuming, of course, he *had* been waiting and not just working. But there was no doubt about the way he'd said it. '*I'll wait*!'...almost like a threat. Plus he could easily have done his work in his suite.

The thought made her apprehensive. She'd kept him waiting. Actually, now that he was all waited out, she'd stood him up and she didn't like doing that to anyone. Maybe she ought to still meet him and explain, but after hesitating for so long, she'd begun to feel flustered. And flustered wasn't the best way to face him. Maybe tomorrow, she thought, when he wasn't upset.

*Upset.* She almost laughed. Thane struck her as a man whose emotions would run on extremes. Once you managed to push him past impassive, he'd be at boiling point. He certainly wouldn't waste his time on such tepid emotions as being "upset."

Satisfied with this latest thought, she stayed out of sight until he disappeared into the elevator. Then she waited five minutes before taking the stairs.

&#x2767;

The next day, Naaki made sure to complete her tasks as quickly as possible. Even so, by the time she was done, it was close to seven. She decided to take the elevator. Get in, get out, and go straight to her room. That was the plan. No diversions and no risk of dinner or after-dinner-drinks invitations. She tapped her foot and hummed to herself. Two more days and she'd be back at home ready again to conquer the world. And far away from Thane Aleksander who made her whole body tingle with awareness whenever he was near.

She felt optimistic. She'd gathered a lot of good information for her report and there were two more job interviews lined up. Certainly not as exciting as MIA, but good opportunities nonetheless. She wasn't going to mess those up as she'd done with MIA.

*Come on, Come on, Come on,* she entreated the elevator as it seemed to hover somewhere between the second and third floors.

But it was too late.

She sensed him before his purposeful footsteps became audible. Her heart stopped for a couple of seconds, and she closed her eyes briefly. She swallowed, trembling

74

slightly at the idea of having to share the elevator with him. Too late to choose the stairs now, though. This would be a good time for the floor to open up and swallow her whole.

He came to stand at her side giving her a full whiff of his cologne and the more intoxicating "essence of Thane" underneath. After she'd breathed in and out once, her pulse raced with renewed life as she waited for what he had to say about yesterday. Now she wondered if hiding had been a good idea.

こうこう

After a moment, Thane asked, "Short day?"

She shot a glance his way without actually looking at him. "Yes."

Thane noticed the tension in her shoulders and the quickening of her breath. He remained silent for a while, choosing to be impassive. After all, he wasn't in the same celebratory mood as yesterday.

"I've never seen you take the elevator."

She did the quick glance thing again. "I usually take the stairs."

He nodded, wondering if it was for fun or exercise. A few seconds passed as he took in

Empi Baryeh

the sight of her shapely legs in modest court shoes; practical for her current duties. Her skirt was just about knee-high with a coat that sat comfortably on the rise of her firm, round derriere. She took in a deep breath, and he caught the movement of her breasts heaving and settling back as she exhaled. She tapped her feet as if to a tune, but he could see beyond that. She was nervous. Well, she should be—after standing him up. Not that it mattered. It hadn't been a date.

"After you." He stepped aside for her when the elevator's doors finally opened.

She looked at him briefly and the expression in her eyes gave him pause. She actually looked worried. The question was, why? Not that it bothered him. Why should it?

Inside the elevator, Thane took his place somewhat behind her, availing himself to a good view of her award-winning butt. Still, he noticed how she clutched her bag. She was definitely anxious about something. Did she, perhaps, feel uncomfortable around him? None of his business, he had to remind himself again. What was it about this woman that made him want to get involved? It wasn't like him at all.

76

He repressed the urge to probe. But when she continued to count the floors as the elevator rose, it began to bug him that she'd be nervous around him. She wasn't in any danger in his presence. He swore and did—as it turned out—the stupidest thing he could have done. He stepped towards her, pulled the red button and the elevator jerked to a halt.

The look in her eyes turned to full blown terror. "Oh my God," she cried, gripping the elevator's side bars. She was scared.

All thought flew out of Thane's mind as he held her. She wasn't breathing. "Naaki, what's wrong?"

"Enclosed spaces—" she gasped.

Thane swore again. "Look at me," he pleaded, and when she still seemed agitated, he made it a command. "Naaki, look at me!"

The sound of her name seemed to catch her attention, and she met his eyes.

"That's it," he coaxed. "Listen to me. You're not in an enclosed place."

She made a move to raise her eyes from his.

"No! Look into my eyes," he said. He hadn't done this before and was going on pure instinct. He figured if her mind didn't dwell on her surroundings, she'd calm down.

"Imagine yourself in an open space and breathe."

For a few seconds she held his gaze but she didn't seem to be breathing. "Breathe for me...please."

Finally, his words seemed to sink in and she began to take in deliberate breaths. When she appeared relatively calm, he picked up her bag and lifted her into his arms, then he released the red button. All the while, his eyes never left hers.

*Of all the*—claustrophobia? Somehow it seemed an odd condition for someone as assertive as her.

He didn't care, he decided. Right now, he just needed to maintain eye contact without dwelling on how well her curves fit or how soft her skin felt. His job was to deposit her safely at her door and walk away—no matter how tempting the idea of laying her in a bed.

At least that was the plan...before her breathing settled down and his escalated, before the scared look dissolved,

and her eyes filled with complete trust. By the time he eased her feet back to the floor in front of her door, it didn't matter that there was no bed around. He was lost in those sexy brown eyes and could hear only the beckoning of her lips. Heeding the voice only he could hear, he lifted her face and kissed her—soundly enough to draw a deep moan from her. Music to his heart. He felt all his defenses begin to shatter as he delved deeper, coaxing a response from her. In the end, he had to let her go, but when he did, reluctantly, he didn't pull back too far.

She was leaning against him, her eyes closed and her lips puckered, as if expecting more. He swallowed, wanting to give more. Stunned by his own reaction, he held her long enough to ensure she was steady on her feet, then said what he'd intended all along. "You owe me a drink!"

# CHAPTER 5

Naaki opened her eyes and he was gone. Just like that. If she'd been hit by a truck and dragged along a few meters, she'd have recovered faster. Completely dumbfounded, she forgot to breathe until sheer self-preservation forced a sharp intake of air. Even so, her mind remained blank, capable of forming just one thought. *Thane kissed me!* She couldn't wrap her mind around it. Her knees felt so weak, she could barely find enough strength to pick up her bag and enter her room.

Shutting the door behind her, she secured the lock with shaky fingers. Something bubbled inside her, something pure and mysterious that made her feel giddy and inexplicably alive. Thane had kissed her, and it was as if she'd never been kissed until now. She felt whole though she'd had no knowledge of being incomplete.

Without thinking, she stopped in front of the mirror by the closet and inspected her lips, needing to know whether they looked as swollen as they felt. *No.* They didn't look swollen—just thoroughly kissed. She moved a couple of stunned steps and paused again, this time at the adjoining door. Of its own accord, her body leaned against the panel and a smile teased the corners of her lips. Gradually, shock gave way to yearning, and yearning metamorphosed to aching.

She'd never known kisses could melt you, never met a man who could kiss you till you turned to wax. This was how kisses were supposed to be. An epiphany. How come she'd never known this feeling before? It had started in her toes and melted its way through her legs, pooling in her lower stomach, then it burst into flames that set her heart ablaze. And she'd wanted more.

Did Thane have some special magic? Was he just exceptionally good at everything he did? How did one get good at kissing? Practice? It had to be, because there was no way his kissing skills were based purely on talent. How many women had he practiced on? How many had melted at his caress? How many, like her, had wanted more?

Finally, she fell upon her bed, convinced she had to stay away from him. With such lethal kisses, Thane Aleksander was a dangerous man. She wasn't going to be one of the many women Thane got to practice his kissing on. Oh, but what a kiss.

ↄ৸ↄ৸

He'd kissed her. *Kissed* her! What the hell was he thinking? Thane tossed his jacket aside and yanked off his tie. *Of all the stupid—*

Raking his fingers through his hair, he muttered a curse. The urge to hit something assaulted him with a force that should have surprised him. The perfect punching bag would have been his own body, since it was apparent that he needed to pound some sense into his skull. Right now, the only thing pounding was his heart as it threatened to burst out of his chest, throbbing partly out of anger but mostly from his pulsing desire.

Damned if he didn't still want her in his arms. She made him feel like a teenager— and not in a good way. Vulnerable wasn't a desired state of mind as far as he was concerned. He sat down with the adjoining door in full view, still unable to comprehend how he'd dropped his guard. How he seemed so *willing* to let down his defenses around her.

He'd panicked in the elevator, allowed himself to be captivated. He'd worried about her, touched her as if he cared. She'd kissed him back, moaned against his lips and his knees had gone weak. He could have made love to her right there in the lobby. He could *care* about her, and caring was the last thing he could afford to do.

Yet staring at the door, the only thing he could think of was how his name would sound on her lips when she cried it out in a deep, long moan.

*Two doors*. Physically, that was the only obstacle preventing him from finding out. But there were other—more compelling— reasons why he should stay away from her. None of them explained why she excited him just by being. Not that it should matter. *No dating*. That was the rule. He needed to keep that in mind at all times. As it was, he'd already risked too much of himself by kissing her.

She'd been scared, and he'd taken advantage of her.

*Dammit.* Naaki wasn't a woman you got involved with on a whim. He needed, at all cost, to avoid her—the woman who'd so easily brought him to his knees, who'd caused his body to come alive and made him want—

Just want.

❧❧❧

The perspiration cooled Thane's skin even though his hands still felt rather warm from the weights he'd been lifting. He dabbed his forehead with the towel hanging over his shoulder.

With conference activities going on, he had a hard time taking his mind off Naaki and the enigmatic effect she was beginning to have on him. Two days after kissing her, he still felt like he was holding his breath at the prospect of seeing her again.

He could hear music from the pool area. The open doors revealed a cocktail function, and information arrows directing guests to the event indicated that it was the Pan-African conference. He slowed down hoping he would see her, and when he did, his breath caught.

She wore modest jewelry with a cocktail dress, the color of deep red wine. Even in that understated, *single* color, she still managed to be the brightest spot in the array of conference delegates. If he were dressed properly he'd have asked her to join him for a drink. Again.

He swore under his breath. What was the matter with him? That woman standing there looking sexy as hell was the last thing he needed right now. He knew he had to leave, but somehow he lingered, watching her laugh and talk with a group of delegates. A smile came to his lips, and warmth spread through him from somewhere in the vicinity of his heart.

At that moment, she turned and saw him. She smiled, before surprise registered, then she directed her attention back to the group.

Thane turned towards the elevators. He should probably return to the gym, but he'd need a little more than another workout to snuff the attraction he felt for her. That realization didn't stop him from jabbing the button for his floor or watching her until the doors slid shut.

That was when he noticed he had a hard on—big time. He bit back another swear word. He'd always had control but this—this one had taken him by surprise. Now, he couldn't wait for the conference to end. Being so close to her, knowing he could find her next door, and the huge possibility of bumping into her didn't help matters. Unless, of course, if he was thinking of his growing desire to bed her.

Returning to his room, he did what he should have done right from the start. He walked straight to his briefcase, and pulled out the letter he'd been holding on to for the past few days. He took resolute steps toward the adjoining doors, and then slipped the envelope underneath. Going back to his work, he tried not to keep glancing over at the letter that officially made her unattainable.

లిలిలి

By the time Naaki returned to her room, exhaustion permeated her every pore. After five days of waking up early, going to bed late and running around in between, she was glad the conference had finally ended. The cocktail party had been a success, but she was ready to shed her clothes, take a long bath and crawl into bed. Kicking off her shoes, she sighed gratefully as her aching feet sank into the soft carpet. Tossing her bag with enough force to land it on the bed, she went to the bathroom to run a bath.

She took her time cleaning her makeup, because in her tired state, even such a task was arduous. Thane was probably sleeping, she thought, then wondered why her mind would drift to him at all. She shook her head. The answer to that question was obvious. Seeing him today brought back the memory of his kiss, making her lower abdomen stir with warmth.

In his arms, she felt like she'd discovered something of herself, something that was both soothing and disconcerting. She still hadn't been able to put it into words, nor had she managed to explain why catching a glimpse of him earlier on made her so happy. He could potentially destroy her immediate professional future, yet she couldn't erase the image of him in his gym outfit, with his wet hair clinging to his head. She'd wanted to walk over and dip her fingers in his hair.

She shed her clothes and hung them on the towel rail, then lowered herself carefully into the warm water. She moaned as her body absorbed the water's heat and her aching muscles began to unwind.

Thirty minutes later, she stepped out of the tub feeling more relaxed, but still tired. The only thing on her mind was curling up under the sheets and having a dreamless sleep. Just as she was about to sink onto the double bed, a white envelope caught her eye. Frowning, she turned. Curiosity propelled her towards it. She wondered briefly if it had slipped from Thane's documents, but there wasn't enough space between the carpet and the door. He had to have pushed it through himself. Picking it up, she flipped it over, immediately noticing the MIA logo and her name.

With a sudden energy boost, she ripped the envelope open. Her shaky hands pulled out the two-page letter.

"Dear Miss Tabika," she read. "We are happy to inform you..."

Her jaw dropped and her eyes widened with every word. Adrenaline surged in her veins. She held the letter with both hands as if afraid it might disappear from her grasp and devoured the words, going over them once again to confirm what she'd just read, and then a third time to ensure she hadn't missed anything. Finally, she sank onto the bed, her whole body pulsing with renewed energy. Resting her hand on her chest, she tried to quell the excitement. It was like trying to block an active volcano, and her elation soon erupted into a joyous shriek, which dissolved into laughter as she did a victory dance.

She tossed herself into the bed, as the laughter subsided. Her eyes twitched as a light film of tears misted in them, surprising her. She'd never come close to crying happy tears, but she was suddenly overcome with emotion. It was as though she'd been suffocating, and unexpectedly, she could breathe again.

The urge to share the news with someone seized her, but at close to midnight, neither her mother nor Pat would be awake. Crazily enough, they weren't the ones she wanted to talk to. The voice she really wanted to hear belonged to the man who'd just given her the happiest moment of her life. To think he could just as easily have handed her the exact opposite. Such was the power he had over her life. She could accuse him of many things, but prejudice wasn't one of them.

He'd just proven he could set aside his personal feelings and make an objective decision. Well, so could she. In fact, right now she felt only positive things toward Thane.

After several minutes, the adrenaline surge dissipated and she was, once again, exhausted from her long day. Her eyes felt heavy. Placing the letter safely on the nightstand, she crawled under the sheets. She used her last ounce of energy to send Pat a short text message, "*Fila, nkɔmɔ.*" The combination of Pidgin and Akan conveyed a stronger message of juicy news than their English equivalent. Just because her friend was asleep didn't mean she couldn't share the information.

She let out a heavy, contented sigh and closed her eyes. She fell asleep with a smile.

ை

Her phone rang at seven in the morning, drawing Naaki out of dreams of her first week at MIA. Answering it, she made sure her voice sounded drowsy, even though she was already fully awake.

"Spill it," Pat said and received a chuckle from Naaki.

"Are you aware it's only seven in the morning?"

"Are you aware you sent me a text message at midnight, knowing I'd be itching to hear the good news when I woke up?"

Unable to tease as she'd intended, Naaki blurted out, "I got the internship at MIA."

Pat shrieked, and Naaki followed with one of her own. Seven or so hours of sleep hadn't diminished her excitement. They talked for nearly thirty minutes before saying their goodbyes. After that, Naaki called her mother and talked for just as long. By the time she was done with those two calls, she was buzzing with positive energy. She took a shower, dressed and packed her things.

An hour later, she locked her bags and set them by the bed. She intended to come back for them after breakfast and proceed to check out. She didn't pause or even glance when she passed Thane's door, although the urge to knock was almost overwhelming. She had to remind herself that they weren't just two guests in a hotel anymore. He was her boss. The thought stopped her in her tracks. She'd kissed her boss! Well...he wasn't her boss yet—not for a few days. Besides, *he'd* kissed her. *He* should be the one feeling guilty. So there.

As she descended the stairs to the restaurant, she noticed several tables occupied by conference delegates. She scanned the room, searching for one she could share. Then she saw Thane and froze. He was reading a newspaper while sipping a beverage. Her heartbeat shot up as she contemplated turning back. Breakfast could wait till she returned home.

Just as she made up her mind, he looked up. His eyes were fixed on hers as he put down the paper and sat back. He tilted his head as if waiting for her next move. A mixture of excitement and indecision battled for dominance before she finally took a step toward him. Trapped in his gaze, she couldn't have done otherwise. As she approached, his eyes never left hers.

"Good morning," she said when she reached the table, surprised at how steady her voice sounded.

"Hi," he replied.

Her nerves on edge, she watched his lips settle into a slight smile. She didn't have to wonder what they tasted like anymore. Ignoring the butterflies fluttering her stomach, she fought to keep her chin up. She should have been telling him in no uncertain terms how wrong it was to kiss her, how unacceptable it was to use his lips to turn her legs to wax.

"Care to join me?" he asked, pulling out one chair.

Nodding, she sat down. She didn't trust herself to talk. Not after catching sight of a light film of black hair exposed through the unfastened top button of his shirt. Her fingers itched to feel that hair. Tearing her eyes away from it, she concentrated on placing her handbag on the chair next to her. If her face grew any warmer, she would need to go and take a dip in the pool.

"Congratulations on joining the team," he said, seemingly oblivious to the effect he had on her. "Assuming you're going to accept our appointment."

"Thank you. Yes, I will be accepting the appointment." As if she had a choice. She didn't say what she was thinking, though. No sense in giving him a reason to withdraw the decision.

She wanted to ask herself what she was doing having breakfast with Thane, but all she could do was marvel at how wonderful he looked with his shirt sleeves folded up and a button undone. The fact that he was her soon-to-be boss didn't seem to be registering on her wayward mind.

As she poured herself a cup of tea, she said, "You know, about the drink...I didn't actually say, yes."

His smile brightened before he laughed. "But you didn't actually say no, and you don't strike me as a woman who would leave a 'no' to interpretation. You certainly aren't afraid to say what you think."

An image of their first meeting—undoubtedly what he was referring to—flashed in her head. "I don't usually stand people up either."

"I didn't think so," he said. "Perhaps it was special treatment for me."

Surprised by his bold assertion, she turned to look at him. His eyes, which betrayed no emotion, were focused intently on her, and they held a conviction that dared her to question him. If he wanted to make her feel bad, he was succeeding.

"I—I'm going to get some fruit from the buffet table." She didn't wait for a response before escaping from his scrutiny, hoping he didn't see the unease in her eyes. She'd have to think up ways to avoid him at the office.

# CHAPTER 6

Naaki *never* woke up before six o'clock—any day. But this morning wasn't an ordinary occasion. It was the first day of her internship, and she was wide awake by five-thirty. The appointment letter lay on the bedside table. Now, she remained in bed, bubbling with excitement and trying to suppress the nerves that threatened to unsettle her stomach. This was her dream job. The enormity of it hit her, which explained why she continued to stare at the letter, reluctant to start the day. What if she blew it? It was a miracle she had gotten the job at all.

In her enthusiasm, she'd called and cancelled all but one of the new interviews scheduled during the conference. "Over-commitment to one cause" would be her undoing. At least that's what Gyamfi had once said. It was one of the kinder expressions he'd used. On his bad days, he called it her "narrow-focused ambition," and "putting all her eggs in one basket."

There was also the fact that she didn't feel ready to face Thane yet, to have him be her boss, a position which gave him the power to confirm or refute Gyamfi's assessment of her. And he'd already offered his opinion on it. '*That was rather foolish, wasn't it?*' His words after the interview shouldn't have affected her, but they did. Worse, they hurt, and she hadn't even known him.

She wanted him to be impressed with her work, her intellect. The only way of making it happen was to get out of bed and be the best intern MIA—and Thane Aleksander for that matter—had ever seen. Was there a way to switch off the butterflies in her stomach when he stared into her eyes? She didn't *want* to be affected by him. She certainly didn't have the same effect on him or surely he'd have mentioned the kiss. *That kiss.* Was it so easy for him to forget?

Aside from the remark, at breakfast last week, about speaking her mind, he'd been all business while explaining the few issues for which she'd needed clarification.

She'd spent the past week completing her presentation, which Thane would undoubtedly ask for at some point today. There was no sense in procrastinating and letting all that work go to waste.

With that thought, she dragged herself out of bed, taking an hour to get ready and have breakfast. Her mother called like clockwork at seven to wish her luck on her first day. Pat, still in Cape Coast, also called to boost Naaki's morale and to find out what she'd finally decided to wear. After her friend's pep talk, Naaki felt confident once again. By the time she stepped out of the house, her focus was firmly on the experience she'd be getting from working at the agency, which was what internships were about, after all.

∽∾∽

Concentrating proved to be a Herculean task. Thane had just gotten off a conference call with a client and was putting together a brief report. It had taken a harrowing hour, but he'd managed to turn a skeptical client into a one-year partner. He hoped their lawyers could finalize the details and have a contract drawn up by the end of the week.

With Mr. Boateng out on a family emergency for the next few days, Thane was on his own. He welcomed the challenge, although having been in the country a little over a fortnight, he definitely would prefer to have someone on the inside assisting him. That fully accounted for his eagerness to see Naaki, the reason why he couldn't concentrate. He looked forward to going through her presentation, but he couldn't deny the tinge of excitement at the prospect of laying his eyes on her. He could think of a few other things he would have liked to lay on her.

He sat back for a moment remembering her voice and her deep brown eyes with those long, dark lashes that swept the air when she blinked. He kept reminding himself not to think of her in any way that was less than professional, but he couldn't prevent the thumping of his heart when his thoughts more than occasionally paused on her.

After sending the email report, he checked the stock market, pleased to find his portfolio doing quite well. He made a mental note to call Toni over the weekend. Antonia

Lucas, his financial advisor, was one of the very few true whizzes in the industry. Thane and Toni met in the days of the dot.com bubble when he'd been thinking of outsmarting the market and getting out when the getting was still good. One didn't have to be Warren Buffet to know to be careful with new technology and internet stocks, but Thane had been lucky. He'd sold his for a neat profit just before the bubble burst. With Toni's expert counseling, he'd made himself a small fortune. Now, he stuck with more traditional, safer stocks.

After checking his personal mail again and finding nothing new, he logged off. There was nothing left except to wait for Naaki.

ꞶꞶꞶ

Naaki felt rather jittery approaching the building. The gleaming BMW in the lot spiked her nervousness a notch. She remembered seeing Thane drive off in it the first day she'd met him. Why couldn't he have been out of office like any normal executive?

Feeling about as anxious as the day of her interview, she entered the building. The receptionist, an older woman, who wore too much makeup, gave her a pleasant smile.

"We've been expecting you. I'm Aku," she said after Naaki had introduced herself. "Please have a seat."

Naaki wondered if anyone had ever bothered to show her how to use the makeup to enhance her features instead of trying to clog her pores.

She sat down and took in her surroundings. The ivory walls displayed a large version of the agency's logo and a couple of paintings. Nothing special. Just like the plain blue wall-to-wall carpeting. Everything was nice but not breathtaking. As part of the team now, she felt justified to make such assessments. If she owned this company, she'd make sure the reception area held an ambience that conveyed to potential clients the kind of quality they could expect from MIA. The same way a good hotel made you feel when you walked into the main lobby.

Aku picked up the phone and announced Naaki's arrival. Turning back to her, she said, "He'll be with you shortly."

Who would be with her shortly? Mr. Boateng or Thane? A minute hadn't passed, it seemed, when Thane entered the reception area. *Oh my.* Wearing a light blue shirt and dark blue tailored pants, he looked good enough to eat. He extended a hand.

"*Akwaaba*," he said, his accent making it sound funny.

She laughed and was surprised to discover she didn't need to force it. She admired the effort to speak what was likely his first Akan word. In fact, if she were to admit it, she found it attractive, but she wasn't admitting anything. Her skin tingled as she shook his hand.

"Thank you, Aku," he said to the receptionist before turning back to Naaki. "I hope you've had enough time to rest after the conference."

"I think so." She *hoped* so.

"Terrific. Agency work can be very demanding." He gestured for her to follow him. "Come this way."

Thane ushered her into the boardroom and signaled for her to sit down. He handed her a folder, saying it contained a few helpful articles and a schedule for her first month.

"Some of the items were required by the Chartered Institute of Marketing," he said. "I'll give you a couple of minutes to flip through."

Naaki opened the folder, noting some interesting articles that she looked forward to reading. Amazingly, the anxiety she'd experienced earlier had faded away. She was relaxed and eager to get started. Thane hadn't lied. From her schedule, it appeared her days were going to be full.

"Nervous about starting your internship?" he asked, bringing her attention back to him.

"I'm more excited than nervous," she confessed. A shiver slithering through her spine made her wonder for an instant if her answer was entirely true. Sitting opposite him, trying not to stare or feel intimidated, she wasn't completely sure it had anything to do with the job.

"We developed something I like to call 'buddying.' In your first few weeks you'll rotate from department to department. You'll have an agency buddy who'll work closely with you to give you practical training of what each department is about." He smiled. "I believe that's a whole lot more effective than any theoretical mumbo-jumbo."

It all sounded so interesting. She hoped she wasn't grinning like a fool.

"As you can see from the schedule, your first week is with management," he went on.

"Unfortunately Mr. Boateng is off for a few days, so you're stuck with me."

So much for thinking up ways to avoid him.

"Any questions?"

"Just one. Will I buddy with Mr. Boateng at all?"

"When he returns, absolutely," he said. "It's going to be a busy day for you. I'll give you a tour of the office, and introduce you to the staff and the various departments. Then we'll have a brainstorming session with the strategic planning team to give you data for your project."

"Okay."

"You'll be presenting to the client on Friday."

Her eyes widened in surprise. Friday? As in, *this* Friday? "I will?"

He chuckled. "Don't worry, I'll be there, too, but consider this your baby."

"All right." She hoped her answer didn't sound as skeptical as she felt. Of course, she wanted to dazzle the client with her ideas—*her* ideas—but now that the ball had been thrown in her court by *über* businessman Thane Aleksander, she didn't know if she was quite ready. What if his expectations were too high?

There was no time to speculate on that as he stood. "Come on. Let's get your day started."

With Thane leading the way, they headed out of the room. First, they visited an open plan office, which housed all of the departments apart from Creative and Finance. The big hall had clusters of desks, and hanging from the ceiling over each cluster was a sign indicating a department name. This room was a lot more interesting than the reception area. There were ad cuttings and products samples, at some stage or other of the advertising cycle, Naaki assumed. There was a sense of purpose to the voices on the phone and in the expressions on the faces of those staring hard at their computer monitors. A large copier by the door hadn't stopped printing since they entered. She was going to enjoy working here, she decided.

As they walked in, a woman, fair complexioned and wearing an expensive-looking suit, had just gotten off the phone, fuming. She spat out the F-word three times, adding, "Those media idiots."

Naaki frowned at the swear word and hesitated as she realized they were approaching the woman whom Thane introduced as the media manager, Grace. There was nothing graceful about the words that came out of her mouth.

"What's happening, Grace?" Thane asked, looking unperturbed, while Naaki held her tongue with effort.

Grace was more than happy to announce her displeasure at the wrong placement of an ad in the papers.

"Our client's brand sells health and vitality products, and those people placed the ad next to the obituaries. Dead people. Who does that?" She threw up her arms in frustration. "And they keep saying the editor is not available." Turning to Naaki, she said, "Nice to meet you. Don't worry, I'm usually very nice, but three years on this job and you'll begin to swear, too."

Naaki doubted that very much. She glanced quickly at Thane, silently begging him to move on. Thankfully, he complied. She met two others in the media department before moving a few cubicles over where she was introduced to the three people in the Strategic Planning department. Thane chatted with them a moment as if he'd known them longer than a couple of weeks. Try as she may, she couldn't help the weakness she felt in her knees when he looked at her with eyes that appeared to see through to her soul.

Everyone was dressed in business casuals except for the two Account Executives she met next—AEs or 'suits' as they were called in advertising circles. Thane mentioned briefly that he'd started working as a "suit." Their sharp appearances paled compared to his.

They passed through the Finance office and proceeded to the creative studio.

It was a larger space than the open plan office. Right in the middle of the studio was a set of comfortable chairs and a table. There were no cubicles here—just designer desks for the five people sitting at their iMacs. None of them glanced their way.

Naaki found herself whispering, "It's so quiet in here."

He leaned in slightly as if to divulge a secret. "The walls are sound proof."

In one corner sat a guy whose age Naaki couldn't particularly guess. Thane introduced him as Jeremy, the creative director. He was good-looking, with curly brown hair, although he had a bit of a gut. Jeremy assessed Naaki as he took her hand.

"Pleasure to meet you," he said. "You're a sight for sore eyes."

He didn't let go of her hand immediately. There was something unsettling in the way he surveyed her and rubbed the back of her hand with his thumb. Naaki hoped her buddying period with Jeremy would be kept to a minimum.

Surprise—and relief—shot through her when Thane touched her elbow, pulling her away. Maybe spending her first week with the boss wasn't a bad idea, after all.

Subsequent to meeting each person, she stood and appraised the room with a look of pure glee on her face.

"I like this room," she whispered. "It's so quiet, so serene and peaceful."

"Yeah, creative rooms tend to be that way. I like to call it calm chaos. This is where you see the planning and brainstorming come together."

"So will I get to buddy with someone in this room as well?"

He nodded. "You'll have over a couple of weeks here. I'm hoping you'd be able to spend a few days at a time with each art director. They all have very different styles and competencies that you might want to talk to them about."

"Including Jeremy?"

His features darkened a shade at the question, making her wonder if he'd misunderstood her motive for asking. "Including Jeremy."

Perhaps she was jumping to conclusions about Jeremy. After all, he wouldn't be here if he wasn't good at what he did. Injecting a smile into her voice, she asked, "What about reception work?"

When Thane glanced at her, his features softened again. He matched her smile. "You never know. Come on, you'll love the next room."

It was definitely some sort of storage area. Not for supplies, though. This was where they kept clippings of old ads. Thane stood aside and allowed her to walk in first. The smile on her face became broader as she approached a stack of archived adverts. She picked one up and gasped.

"I remember this." She held it up for him to see.

It was an A2 sized board with an artwork for a billboard pasted on it. It showed a woman with a child on her back, and she was casting a vote. At the bottom of it was written:

*Candidate A: 4,730,000*
*Candidate B: 4,730,000*
*Too Bad You Didn't Vote.*

It was a simple concept. In truth, the difference of one vote would mean a runoff, but it made for a poignant piece of communication—one she loved. He smiled with her as she explained about the concept.

"It was a great campaign," she said, then her excitement toned down in self-awareness when she realized he wasn't looking at the ad. He was watching her, making her conscious of how alone they were in the small storage room.

Ignoring the mounting tension, she said, "I—I know it means nothing to you, but it was the millennium. You had Y2K; we had the chance to change governments through the ballot box for the first time ever. Some people thought it couldn't happen or it wouldn't make a difference. Others were trying to get used to the idea of having a say. And this campaign said 'you can do it. It matters that *you* voted.' It was huge. Many people began to care after the 'too bad you didn't vote' ads."

She laughed, realizing she was getting carried away. He didn't laugh, but continued to look at her intently. Naaki's gaze faltered.

"So did you vote?" he asked, reaching for the clipping. His voice sounded low and deep. It did things to her that made her want to close her eyes and simply listen to him speak.

"I was only seventeen," she said by way of explanation before releasing it to his grip. Though their hands didn't touch, his closeness made her shiver. She redirected her attention to another clipping.

❧❧❧

Thane stood back and gave her space as she lost herself in the old ads, some of them obviously meaning more to her than others. He was caught up in watching the occasional look of nostalgia that came across her face as she rediscovered several old ads. She seemed to connect with some on an emotional level. Her smile had started small, brightening with every new piece she picked until it was bright enough to light up the room. Thane found himself wishing he could share the experience with her, and not feel so left out from her world. But he couldn't be a part of it, so he occupied himself with the visual feast that she was.

She had her back to him and he took private pleasure in absorbing her curves. *Those legs*—those long, shapely legs. In this climate, nylons weren't a fashion accessory, and her bare legs only served as nature's new torture device—tormenting him for wanting what he couldn't have. Like her award-winning bottom that he wouldn't have minded getting his hands on. Her small waist accentuated her curvy hips and made her all the more alluring.

*Phew.* Did someone turn up the heat? Thane shook himself back to reality, sounding a firm mental reminder that she was off limits. What would it take to get the message to sink in?

Maybe he ought to set up a "no company dating" rule—make it official. Besides, he was sure she wouldn't appreciate all the men in the office coming down on her like dogs after a bitch in heat.

The image of Jeremy, all but drooling when he'd introduced Naaki, came to mind. Thane had been seized by an urge to protect her. From what, he didn't know. The creative director's words and leering had bugged him more than it should have. Jeremy made no secret about finding Naaki attractive. Thane couldn't fault the guy. There was no red-blooded male on the planet who could pass by and not notice her exotic beauty. But the idea of someone pursuing her—right under his nose, no less—left a bad taste in his mouth. *Note to self: keep an eye on Jeremy.* He wished he could avoid having Naaki "buddy" with the guy, but he couldn't. Not if he wanted her to learn, which was the only reason for her being there in the first place. He needed to keep that in mind.

He noticed immediately when she looked pensive. "What are you thinking?"

"Oh, nothing." She hesitated then looked up at him. "I mean, the reception area has the agency logo and two paintings on the wall, and they're nothing special. If we framed some of these great works and put them on the walls, it would give more character to the reception area. You know, a place that tells you immediately as you enter, 'this is MIA;

this is what we do.'" She shook her head. "Never mind, I—"

"No," he replied, taking a step to where she stood. Something about her scent made him think of standing in a field of wild herbs. How come he'd never imagined wild herbs could smell so feminine? "I agree the reception area looks rather plain. It definitely needs a makeover. I'd been thinking along the lines of a mural, but I believe you've just struck gold with this idea. We need to turn it into a cozy yet sophisticated space that is still MIA."

"Yes," she replied, looking surprised.

Did she think he wouldn't catch her drift? He saw and caught more things about her than he cared to admit. She put the board in her hand back where she found it. As she turned, she tripped on a wire and grabbed for him in reflex just as he caught her. God, she was beautiful. Even his sorry heart could recognize it, despite the fact that dating wasn't on his agenda anymore.

"Careful." His voice had turned husky so quickly he didn't recognize it himself. Heat emanated from where her hand had landed on his chest, and he wished he could return the favor. His hand covered hers, and he let himself enjoy the feel of her soft, small hands in his relatively larger one before tearing her hand away. He swallowed. This wasn't going to be an easy week.

*෴*

For an instant before he released her, Naaki thought he was going to kiss her. Because in that split second when their eyes locked, time vanished, and she'd been aware only of her heartbeat and his...until he pried her hand away and broke the connection.

Heat blazed her cheeks. *Great.* Not only did she find it hard to breathe in his presence, she was clumsy as well. How would she get him to admire her intellect when she was busy tripping over wires? She felt all the more embarrassed when he led her out of the room with his hand lightly resting on her back as though he needed to ensure she didn't make a fool of herself again. She just wished her fingers weren't still tingling from touching his taut chest muscles and that his hand on her back didn't feel so sensual.

# CHAPTER 7

One and a half more days to go, Thane thought. It was past noon on Thursday. He'd survived the last three and a half days. *Barely*. Working so closely with Naaki had tried every ounce of restraint he possessed. He'd never had to fight so hard to keep his hands by his sides or hold his libido in check. A part of him actually *wanted* to fall for temptation. He thought he'd be glad when the time came to pass her on to Account Management. But sitting in his office, elbows propped on the edge of his desk, chin resting on tented fingers, he didn't *feel* happy.

If he discounted his attraction for her and the lightness of heart he experienced in her presence, undeniable chemistry still brewed between them when they worked together.

Thane couldn't remember the last time he'd thought brainstorming and preparing a presentation were invigorating. Her enthusiasm was contagious, but more than that, she understood his ideas and explanations, and wasn't afraid to challenge him when their opinions differed. The ensuing discussions often led to better solutions. Though he enjoyed the support of the whole team, it was having Naaki as his protégé for the week that had given him the extra oomph.

So if he had to hold his breath every time she walked into a room and suffer fantasies he couldn't consummate, then so be it. He glanced at his watch. *Shit.* She was due in his office any minute, and his emotions were running helter-skelter. He had to compose himself, call up some emergency immunity to survive his own weakening resolve. He needed fresh air. Cooped up in his office with nothing to do except anticipate her arrival, explained his quickening pulse and the stirring of his body downstairs. He couldn't have that.

Pushing away from his desk, he bounded to his feet and headed for the door. Just as he stepped out, she rounded the corner and crashed into him, losing her balance on impact. An "oh," sounded from her, papers flew out of her hands as she reached for the nearest thing. Him.

His arms closed around her in reflex as he stepped forward, bracing his legs to support them. He staggered a couple of steps before steadying himself. Her arms were around his neck, her face only inches from his as she stared into his eyes. His throat went dry and his heartbeat shot through the roof.

As he straightened up, she fell against him, her breasts colliding with his ribs. His body required no further encouragement to come fully alive. Thankfully, that part of him wasn't touching her, so he was spared the embarrassment of her finding out exactly how much she affected him.

"Sorry," she panted, her eyes still round with shock. "I wasn't paying attention."

Thane's words caught in his throat and he swallowed. It took a moment for his mind to register her words since he'd been focusing on the movement of her sensuous lips, rather than the words coming out of them.

It would have been so easy to kiss her, to feel her soft lips part and allow him entry. Had they been anywhere else, he just might have done it. But in the corridors of MIA, anyone could walk in on them, and both their reputations would suffer for his unprofessional behavior. Thankfully, common sense made a much-needed appearance and he heaved her off him.

She blinked rapidly, obviously trying to recover from the incident then squatted to pick up her papers. Instead of doing the sensible thing and walking away, he did the gentlemanly thing and knelt beside her to help. When they were done, he handed his share over, avoiding eye contact.

"Thank you." Her voice was low and breathy, and utterly sensual.

"Wait in my office." Anger at himself made his voice sound a little harsh. "I'll be with you in five minutes."

Without waiting for a response, he made a quick retreat. There was no time to go out for fresh air, so he only went as far as the top of the stairs. When he was out of earshot, he let out a few choice words she wouldn't have approved of. Then taking a deep breath, he closed his eyes and did math in his head.

After a few minutes, with his sanity back to relatively safe proportions, he made his way back to his office. It occurred to him how alone they'd be. Maybe he should lure her out somewhere they'd have an audience, because—God help him—if he made the mistake of kissing her again, he wasn't going to stop.

* * *

Naaki supposed she should be grateful to Thane for giving her a moment to compose herself. The collision had left her off-balance, still wishing for his strong arms to embrace her. She ought to have been watching where she was going. Several deep gulps of air managed to get her heartbeat back to normal, and she took a moment to rearrange her papers. She crossed her legs, hoping to give an impression of complete confidence, but her fingers drumming against the polished surface of the desk were evidence of her edginess. Lord knew how she'd managed to maintain a semblance of level-headedness this whole week.

The sound of the door shutting softly announced Thane's return. Naaki squared her shoulders and waited for him to take a seat.

"Where were we?" he asked in a cheerful voice.

"I revised the document and printed it out." She pushed the proposal forward. "I have a soft copy as well." The rapid thundering of her heart as he flipped through it, clearly indicated more alone time would be beneficial. But tomorrow was the big day, and though the presentation looked good so far, it could use his final input.

He read without talking. Naaki shifted in her seat wondering what was going through his mind. His eyes were on the paper, but she could have sworn he was aware of her every move. A shaky breath escaped her lips. She felt like biting her nails. Would he at least say something? Anything?

Finally, he looked at her. "Are you hungry?"

"Pardon?"

"Do you want to grab lunch?"

Seriously? She wasn't hungry per se but she could eat, although lunch with Thane had "bad idea" written all over it. Not that she didn't want to have lunch with him. Indeed, what bothered her was the fact that she *wanted* to have lunch with him.

"I...uh—" Images of him in a muscle-hugging t-shirt and corduroys flashed across her mind's eye. The way fabric would stretch around his biceps when he made a simple gesture like passing her a plate, or the way she felt so indescribably content in his presence. A meal together would definitely not be a good idea. "I'd like to start working on the presentation, if it's all the same to you."

Immediately, she wondered if she'd made a sensible decision. Breakfast had been so long ago, and she'd have to eat very soon or else—

She pushed that thought out of her mind. She would just have to take a break after an hour or two. For now, she wanted to get started on the work, if only to convince herself that her brain could function as zealously in his presence as her heart seemed to do. Through narrowed eyes, he regarded her with an intense look without speaking for a while. She swallowed, tingling all over with awareness.

Finally, he nodded and placed the proposal before her. "It's all the same to me."

They discussed her proposal. He dissected it, asked questions, took notes and asked more questions. Naaki couldn't help noticing the way he divided the sheet into sections, grouping similar ideas. It was strange to have something so trivial in common with someone. He kept clean short nails, and his fingers moved with the grace of a painter's hands.

When he looked at her, a quiver zipped to the pit of her abdomen and her stomach churned. She caught her breath and tucked in her belly. It couldn't be hunger. Could it? Well, no matter. With Thane so engrossed in taking notes and turning her proposal into something that was actually pitchable to the client, she couldn't take a break now. What time was it anyway?

As if he'd read her mind, he glanced at his designer watch then looked at her. If she wasn't mistaken, there was concern in his eyes.

He stood and went over to a cupboard. "I'm going to make myself some coffee. Are you interested?"

"I don't like the smell of coffee." She wriggled her nose to emphasize the point. Her mind lingered on "interested." Judging by the way her body hummed around him, "interested" might be in the vicinity of what she was feeling.

"Oh boy, left to you alone, Starbucks would be out of business." He flashed a brief smile and rummaged through some drawers.

"Let's see, what else do we have? Hot chocolate?"

"I don't drink hot chocolate. Too much sugar in it." Absurd, she told herself. Of course, she wasn't *interested*, even though he had the most beautiful eyes she'd ever seen, smelled of...pure male, and made her knees go weak when he touched her. "Do you have tea?"

"You drink tea," he stated as if it were the most profound revelation of the year. "Nope, can't say I do." He poked around some more before closing the drawer. "What about water? I have a pitcher in the fridge."

"Yes, I'd like some water, thank you."

Naaki watched his profile as he bent forward to retrieve the water from the small fridge in his office. A bit of his shirt pulled out of his trousers, and that completely ordinary occurrence held so much appeal she had to avert her eyes in order not to be caught ogling. He poured out two glasses and handed her one.

Receiving it, she said, "I thought you were having coffee."

He shrugged. "You don't like the smell of coffee."

Naaki didn't know why his answer affected her as it did. Did her comment really influence his decision not to drink coffee or was it something else? Something like a masculine need to rescue a damsel in distress?

She emptied her glass just as Thane gulped down the last bit of his water. He perched himself back on the seat.

"Tired?" he asked.

*Oh yeah, damsel in distress syndrome.* "No." She wasn't going to let him glorify himself by rescuing her. Besides, he'd already saved her once today. An encore would be too embarrassing.

"Are you sure? We can take a fifteen minute break, or thirty. Whatever you need."

"We might as well finish up the Power-Point if I'm presenting it to the client tomorrow."

"Right." He plugged her thumb drive in place and turned his attention to the computer screen.

Naaki propped one hand against the table determined to conceal her fatigue. She was starving, too, but no way was she going to ask for a break—not after refusing the offer for lunch. She glanced quickly at him as he went through the slides. His brows were furiously creased and his fingers absently twirled the pencil he was holding. He didn't seem tired at all. Obviously he was used to this sort of self-torture.

The taskbar on the computer told her it was almost four. They'd been at work for nearly three hours, yet he sat there as if he'd just started. Her stomach rumbled and she quickly sucked it in again. She could deal with the pain but not the embarrassment of him hearing the insistent growls of her stomach.

"I think this will do," he suddenly said, clicking on "save."

"Great." Now she could get something to eat.

"You did a good job with this, Naaki. Are you ready for the presentation?"

"Yes, I don't think it can get better than it is, thanks to you."

"I just polished it. You did the work." He sat back. "Okay, let's hear it."

"You mean now?"

"Well, I would like to see you rehearse it to me before we meet the client." He moved away from the computer, giving her the feel of an audience. "You did mention the importance of getting it out of the way if you're presenting tomorrow."

Now, he was just mocking her. "Sure." She wasn't going to back out of the challenge. They were close enough to the end. What harm would another few minutes do? "Where do I stand?"

"Right where you are is fine." He spoke with an easy air of a man judging a beauty pageant rather than one listening to a marketing proposal.

She smiled, composing herself. "Good afternoon ladies and gentlemen, my name is—" She paused, taking in a deep breath. "My name is Naaki Tabika, and my colleague is Thane—" Had the room tilted slightly or was it just her?

"Naaki, are you okay?"

"Yes I am, thank you," she replied quickly, but couldn't continue. Instead, her eyes spaced out and she began to fall forward.

✑✑✑

Thane didn't think or he might have talked himself out of rushing to her side, and taking her hand. He helped her to a chair.

"You're trembling," he noted with concern. He hadn't expected her to be jittery about the presentation, but what else could it be? "There's nothing to be nervous about."

"I'm not nervous," she replied, just before tears started rolling from her eyes. She buried her face in her hands.

He'd never considered himself a sucker for tears, but Naaki crying stirred up all sorts of tender feelings in him. He pulled her hands from her face. "What is it, then?"

Even in tears, she was beautiful. Like a magnet, his hand found her face, touching her gently, letting his hand caress her soft cheeks. At the back of his mind, he knew he shouldn't be so close that he could take in her sweet smell.

Had he been man enough, he'd have taken a step back—if only mentally—and found another way to handle the situation. Instead, he felt the urge to smell her more closely, touch his lips to her face, and dry her tears with his kisses. Where was a sprig of mistletoe when he needed one?

"I just need to eat," she said.

"You're crying and shaking because you're hungry?" She'd refused his offer for food so why did he feel like he'd done something wrong? "Do you cry every time you're hungry?"

"I'm not crying. It's just tears," she said stubbornly but her voice sounded weak. "This only happens when I go a long while without food, and I'm not in the habit of starving myself."

Thane shook his head. *No, only when you want a man to feel like a heel.* He should have insisted they ate at some point. He could go with one meal a day, as he often did, but had no right to push her to the limits he pushed himself. He should have thought about her.

Wait a minute, he did. She'd turned down his invitation, as if lunch with him was such bad idea.

Rising to his feet, he ran his hands through his hair in aggravation. "You shouldn't go without food if you know this happens." Why would she do a thing like that? There he went again, *caring.* "That was irresponsible."

Her only response was an apologetic sigh. At least, she had the grace to look contrite. She gave him a tired smile, which was still dazzling, and he felt a little ache in the heart he thought had become numb. He shook his

Empi Baryeh

head as the bulk of his frustration oozed away. He wanted to understand why she could so confidently dress down a stranger for accidentally hitting someone with a banana peel and still be afraid of sharing an elevator with him; and why her body reacted like this when she was hungry. Most importantly, how would the same body respond when it got hungry for him? Why did this all-too-honest woman pull at his heartstrings?

"What do you want to eat?" He intended to feed her even if he had to do it with her kicking and screaming.

"Anything."

Evidently, she now saw the wisdom in eating in spite of his presence. Good.

"My hotel is not far from here. If we order something now it will be ready by the time we get there."

She offered no arguments, and he proceeded to make the call.

လာ

Thane was mesmerized with watching her eat. Her eyes were still a little moist. They'd watered up as soon as she put the first morsel

130

in her mouth but no tears spilled, which was a good thing. Comforting her in his office was a lot different from holding her in his hotel room, and he wasn't about to test his resolve. Not when she looked so huggable and cute—in a very sexy way.

She didn't utter a word for a while. In fact, she hadn't spoken much since they left the office. She'd simply reclined the car seat and leaned back, as if trying to conserve whatever energy she had left. She didn't even complain when, upon arrival at the hotel, he'd held her arm, rather possessively, guiding her. For an unguarded moment, he'd even entertained thoughts of being her man.

When the food arrived, she chose to sit on the carpet, tucking her legs beneath her and propping her back against the chair. Thane was happy to take a place on the carpet next to her, picking at his food and watching her. It wasn't until she'd eaten almost half of what was on her plate that she took a deep breath and looked up at him. His heart did a little dance. Did she just smile or was it his imagination? He shook his head. Of course not. Even if she *had* smiled it was very slight, and it was about the food, not him. Yet if he had a paintbrush he'd have captured that smile on canvas and displayed it to the whole world...no, he'd reserve it for his private collection.

"Thanks for the food," she said and leaned back resting her head on the arm of the sofa.

"Pleasure," he replied and realized it really was. He could watch her eat for a lifetime and not get tired of it. If her tears were so easily wiped away with food, then she was going to be an easy woman to please indeed. But he knew he had no business wanting to please her, wanting to be the one who wiped away her tears.

"You should eat some more."

She smiled, this time more broadly and nodded.

"Why did you do it?" He hated the suspicion in his voice. She'd already mentioned that starving herself wasn't a habit. And she certainly didn't seem to have a problem eating. Still, cynical as it sounded, there had to be something wrong with her. He wanted—needed—a reason to stop falling for her.

She raised innocent eyes to meet his. "Do what?"

He returned her gaze with a pointed look. She knew damn well what. "Why did you stay all afternoon without eating?"

She swallowed, freeing her mouth for an answer. "I didn't think we'd take so long."

He didn't know what he'd expected, but her reply seemed too simple, a half answer. It worried him. Was there something wrong with her? He'd never heard of anyone who could faint from a few hours of hunger. He found himself searching for the right words to say next. "So there's nothing wrong with you medically?"

She shook her head. "I have a fast metabolism. I usually carry a snack, but forgot it on my dining table today."

"But you didn't want to have lunch."

Various emotions clouded her gaze before she spoke again. "I—I wanted to get the presentation over with." She appeared a little guarded. "I get flustered when there's something waiting to be done, and I'm doing something else."

He had a feeling there was more, but he didn't push. After all, it wouldn't do anything for his ego if she admitted to not wanting to have lunch with him. While he was a confident man, he still preferred a boost to his self-esteem over battering it.

Besides, he had more interesting things to do, like stare at her slender arms and the gentle rise and fall of her breasts. She had to be uncomfortable lying on that knot she'd tied her hair into. As if to confirm his suspicions, she inclined her head slightly, leaning off the knot. He inched closer to her unable to resist the urge to let her hair loose.

Not expecting his move, she stiffened as his arm reached behind her. It was slight but he noticed it, along with the sharp intake of air. In a gentle motion, he reached for the scrunchy and pulled it out, releasing her lustrous shoulder-length hair.

To his surprise, she didn't protest, so he dared to comb it out, enjoying the feel of the silky soft tresses between his fingers. Was it just him or did her hair feel different from any other woman's hair he'd touched? Their eyes locked and the air between them heated with tension. In that moment, Thane realized he was looking at the most beautiful woman in the world—one he couldn't have. Even if she weren't a co-worker, what could he offer her in six months? Nothing meaningful—not for someone like her. She was the type of woman you married before you made love to her, in whose eyes you could look and see "forever." But forever was the one thing he couldn't offer. So why did he have his fingers in her hair?

Something shifted within him, and he knew without a doubt that this image of her, with her hair down and her eyes misty, would haunt him forever. As he pushed the hair away from her face, a section of her bangs fell forward almost going into her eyes. He tucked it back in place with the same care he'd used in undoing the bun.

"There," he said with unintended tenderness. "No bangs in your eyes."

She frowned. "Bangs?"

He smiled, realizing the term was probably very American. "The hair hanging over your forehead."

She made a face as if offended by the word.

"What do you call it?" He exhaled heavily, glad for the trivial topic of conversation, which eased away some of the tension.

"It's a fringe," she announced.

He chuckled at her indignation, leaning back against the chair and rolling a lock of hair around his finger. *I say poTAYto, you say poTAHto*, took on a whole new relevance. Silence fell upon them again, but this time it was a comfortable one; the kind that made you want to kick off your shoes on a summer evening and enjoy the breeze, or kiss—just because.

❦❦

Naaki wanted to close her eyes as he played with a tendril of her hair. She knew she should stop him, say something smart to show him she wasn't affected by his closeness, by his touch, but she didn't...couldn't. Maybe it was the way the look in his eyes made her feel like a goddess; or the way his fingers worshipped her hair; or how his eyes said things to her that words couldn't utter; or the manner in which her heart responded with flips she didn't know hearts could do. Until now.

And the problem with it all was, she liked the attention. Even when they first arrived at the hotel, she'd enjoyed the feel of his hand alternating between holding her arm and resting on the small of her back. Everything she'd never have expected from him. And that was exactly it. This *was* Thane Aleksander, obnoxious businessman extraordinaire. He couldn't possibly be the kind of guy to elicit tender feelings from her. Especially when those feeling were so foreign to her. She had to be reading her signals wrong.

When she finally trusted her voice enough, she said, "You're not eating either."

He shook his head, as his lips curved into a grin. "I'm not the one who's starved to tears." Thankfully, though, he withdrew his hand.

She returned his smile. At least he was no longer looking at her with mistrust, like he didn't believe she'd only been hungry. Here was another item for the embarrassing-moments-with-Thane list. She had to admire his control, however. Gyamfi had been close to panic the day the tears came in his presence. At the time, she'd been touched by his frantic efforts to get her fed. Later, she discovered it had been a glimpse into his controlling nature. Thane was handling himself much better. In the face of danger, he would definitely be levelheaded.

He glanced at his watch. "We better finish up quick, so I can take you back to your car."

# CHAPTER 8

Thane couldn't help but be impressed. Naaki was sensational. Wearing one of her trademark colorful suits—and this one fitted like a glove—she had the rapt attention of the four executives from The Mobile Company, a cell phone service provider. All business, she paused on each slide to elaborate. She'd rehearsed well. If he'd had any concerns about trusting her with this project, they were completely gone.

Though he never doubted her ability to deliver, he couldn't help the rush of admiration now bubbling inside. The attraction was still there, threatening to lodge itself in the hidden nooks of his heart, something which frightened him. Yet he constantly found himself flirting with the temptation to unravel her. Could she heal his heart? Shifting his eyes back to the presentation, he realized he'd drifted off momentarily.

Coming to the next to last slide, Naaki took a step forward summarizing her points. "So in a nutshell, this is our proposal for your company for the rest of the year. As you can see, it provides a three-sixty degree solution, making the best use of above- and below-the-line media to achieve your targets."

She hit the arrow button to show the last slide. "Thank you."

As planned, she'd stayed within thirty minutes to allow time for discussion.

She smiled, making eye contact with each of the four executives in turn. "I'll take your questions now."

Thane knew when a client was blown away, and in the case of this group, it was written in their satisfied expressions. A moment of silence followed her invitation for questions, as though they were trying to come up with something to ask. Eventually, the few questions that arose were mostly those Thane had anticipated.

Once the Q&A was over, he took another five minutes to explain the added value of MIA's association with Black & Black, once it was set in stone, and what it would bring to The Mobile Company.

Within another twenty minutes, the meeting was over and they were shaking hands. After promising to review the presentation internally and get back to the agency, Thane and Naaki were led out of the conference room.

The change from the cool conference room temperature to the hot, sunny mid-afternoon air outside caused his skin to prickle uncomfortably. Back in his car, he turned on the air conditioner as soon as they were strapped in. It took a few minutes for the temperature to reach a comfortable level. As his body started to cool down again, he took a deep breath and released it from his mouth.

"I think it went well," he said. "How do you feel?"

He knew firsthand that no matter how much practice you got in school, it didn't compare with actually presenting to a client. In the real world, you couldn't cut corners, and mistakes cost money. But it made each success all the more significant.

She gave him a broad smile, her face glowing. "Good. I was a little nervous at first, but once I started—" She sighed. "—it wasn't as terrifying as I'd thought."

"A bit of nerves is always good. It keeps you from sounding cocky."

Still, in high spirits, she switched on the radio as they began to move out of the parking lot. "What do you want to listen to? Music or news?"

"Music."

"What kind?"

It didn't really matter. Personally, hers was the only voice he wanted to listen to. "You pick."

She settled on a station playing modern jazz. *Good choice.*

"Did you remember your snack today?"

She nodded. "Yesterday was just an off day. I must have been preoccupied with the presentation."

Off-day or not, he wanted to make sure it didn't happen again. While she looked uniquely appealing in tears, the trigger was her going hungry.

"Save your snack for later," he suggested. "Let's eat before returning to the office." It was a friendly invitation, he told himself, not a bid to extend his time with her. Anyone would do the same, so the fact that a sense of joy surged through him meant nothing. "Do you have any suggestions?"

She pursed her lips, thinking. "Have you had Ghanaian food yet?"

"Nope." So far, he'd stuck to what he knew, especially since La Paulanda had an extensive menu. A change would be nice.

"Do you want to try local food?"

"I suppose I'll have to do it sooner or later." He hoped there'd be no surprises. Still vivid in his mind was his first time in Paris when he'd looked forward to his mushroom stuffed with escargot, until it turned out to be snails. "Nothing weird, though. I'm not adventurous when it comes to food."

She laughed, surprise echoing in her voice. "Really?"

"Don't sound so shocked."

She bit her lower lip clearly in an effort to regain composure. "You don't seem like someone who could be timid about anything."

Pride swelled in his chest as though he'd been offered a compliment. Obviously, she'd spent some amount of time thinking about him in order to make such an assessment. "When it comes to food, I like to play it safe.

If my stomach rejects anything, I'm the only one who'll suffer for it."

Even as the words emerged, he wondered why he was sharing something so personal—particularly when it wasn't exactly positive. And more so because he was suddenly filled with a completely illogical desire to impress her. He checked himself. Hadn't he learned his lesson with Arlene? "I'll do local on one condition."

"What's that?"

"I'm not eating anything with a weird name or any dish considered a delicacy."

She laughed. He scowled.

"Okay," she said. "I promise not to make you eat anything you don't recognize."

Good, he thought.

"There's a place close by that makes some of the best local dishes, and the atmosphere is great."

She pointed out directions and within five minutes, they were there. The sign at the entrance was, *Aduane.*

"*A-doo-ane,*" he read. Lately, he often found himself trying to learn stuff about the country. "What does it mean?"

She giggled, pronouncing it the proper way. "The first 'a' is enunciated like the letter and not the sound. *Ei-due-A-ne*. It means food."

He chuckled. "You can't get more literal than that. Straight to the point. No frills." After a few more attempts at pronouncing the name and not getting it quite right, he gave up.

*Aduane* was a one-story facility, he observed, as they got out of the car. He allowed her to lead the way through an indoor restaurant on the first floor to the thatch-roofed lanai. As she climbed the stairs, her skirt crept up a couple of inches, giving him a private moment to fantasize about peeling it off her. She turned abruptly when she got to the landing and he had to look away to avoid revealing his train of thought.

"Where do you want to sit?" Without waiting for an answer, she suggested, pointing towards the solid wood railing, "How about close to the balustrade? It's more airy."

*Balustrade?* He hadn't actually heard someone use that word in conversation. A little reminder that she wasn't your average woman. Her choice of tables suited him fine, so they made their way through some tables and picked one right next to the railing. It overlooked a small garden next to the parking lot. Beyond that, the view was blocked by the tall buildings surrounding the restaurant.

A lively waiter came to welcome them with a now familiar "*Akwaaba.*" Dropping them a menu each, he took their drink orders.

Looking through the list of options, Thane didn't recognize most of the first items, since they weren't in English. Then he spotted something. "What's red-red?"

"Ripe plantain, fried. It goes with black-eye beans in gravy."

He made a face. "Is it good?"

"I like it. Plantain is a cousin of banana, which—"

*Fried bananas?* "I'll pass."

The corners of her lips twitched with a cute smile she tried to hold back. She shook her head and he had a feeling she pitied him for what he was missing. In this one regard, he had no intention of trying to impress her. Not today, anyway.

She moved her finger down the list and pointed out something. "Why don't you choose *Jollof* rice? It's rice cooked in gravy so it comes out orangey and goes with vegetables."

It sounded safe enough. "*Jollof* rice, it is."

They placed their orders when the drinks arrived.

"So what do you think of the atmosphere so far?"

He took a look around. The place was cozy with an African theme. The wooden pillars supporting the roof had intricate designs carved into them. The flagstone flooring was a fascinating tapestry, using colorful stones to create a variety of images that seemed to tell a story. There was local music playing—loud enough to be heard without being intrusive. Fused with the indigenous were modern fixtures to provide a rich ambiance.

"I like it." His gaze returned to her. "This gives me a real taste of your culture."

Her eyes sparkled with delight. "You'll like the food too."

He hoped so. Taking another look around, he studied more of the native identity carved into the furnishing.

"You know." The sound of her voice brought his attention back to the table. "This *is* Ghanaian, but it's manicured. The real cultural experience is out there with the people.

You might never encounter it without try-ing."

She was right. He lived in a hotel, drove the same route to work and back, through an area with very modern architecture. At that rate, he'd still be a stranger by the time he returned home. While he had over five months to go, it was never too early to discover. Moreover, how could he resist when her tone promised an adventure?

"Show me," he said. "I want to see it through your eyes." He reached out to place his hand on hers, then re-thinking the ges-ture, he went for his glass instead.

"I'd be happy to."

The waiter arrived with their orders. "En-joy your meals," he said before leaving.

The rice *did* have a rich orange color. With a serving of assorted vegetables and a fillet of fish on the side, it looked and smelled good. And he was starving. Naaki had chosen red-red, which looked surprising-ly inviting, but he still wasn't tempted. Good thing she didn't offer him a bite. Instead, she fixed him with an expectant stare, waiting for him to taste his food.

*Here goes.* Mixing a portion of rice with veggies, he took a bite of his first Ghanaian

dish. The blend of flavors, with an unexpected tinge of spiciness, was new and delicious. Must have something to do with cooking the rice and gravy together as Naaki had
explained.

"This is really good." His eyes watered as
the heat of the spice hit him in the wrong
place. He reached for his drink and took a
quick sip. "A little spicy, but good."

Her smile disappeared when he coughed.
"Is it too hot? I thought you said mild was
okay." She placed her hand on his shoulder.

Instant heat radiated from where her hand
touched him and his body reacted immediately. "It's fine." He liked spicy food. "Just
went down the wrong way."

He attempted a smile to show her he was
okay, but the warmth seeping through his
shirt from her simple gesture was causing
him more serious problems.

An amused expression quickly replaced
the concern on her face before it too dissolved into a captivating smile. Thankfully,
she dropped her hands off his shoulder, leaving a mixture of disappointment and relief.

As they ate, they discussed the proposed
culture tour. Desire to hold on a little longer
drove Thane to suggest they do it the next

day, Saturday. Feeling completely happy with the arrangement, he didn't mind when the conversation drifted back to work-related issues. Tomorrow would surely come.

ↄ◌ↄ

The next day, as planned, they headed off to town for Thane's culture tour. If the cacophony of color and sound of downtown Accra had been described to him, he'd have thought, "Bring it on." Nothing could beat the human traffic in New York City. He'd have been dead wrong. Thankfully, he had a moment to digest it all from the safe point of Naaki's Beetle. She'd thought it unwise to come in his rented BMW. Now he knew why. Drivers of taxi's and *trotros*—commercial mini buses—drove to a whole different set of laws, all the while honking at their colleagues.

Human traffic, clad in various mixes of western and non-western raiment, was dense and seemingly everywhere. The sounds of people laughing and shouting, some singing, surrounded them. There were quite a few places blasting loud music, as though they were in a competition.

149

Empi Baryeh

As he took it all in, he didn't realize Naaki had stepped out of the car until she rapped at his window. He realized he was reluctant to get out, but a cultural education awaited, and he had the most beautiful tour guide anyone could ask for. He got out, adjusting his shades. He should have brought a cap.

"We're going to do some walking now," she said. "Just blend in. It's going to be fun."

Blend in? Yeah, right. He was the only Caucasian as far as his eyes could see; he couldn't blend in if he tried. No one seemed to pay any special attention to him, however. Perhaps he really was part of the crowd. "Bring it on."

She extended a hand to him. "I don't want to lose you."

And there he was, hoping she just wanted some physical contact. He took the hand she offered, and soon they were meandering through the milling crowd. As they paved their way forward, he began to realize there was some order to the chaos. Like dancing to a new song—it could feel odd until you fell in step. Even the people's gait moved according to some rhythm. It seemed an unconscious thing, but he soon noticed how their steps gradually changed in tune with whatever music could be heard the loudest. He learned to zone in on the closest, absorbing it and moving on to the next as they made their way through.

"Saturdays are busy," Naaki shouted above the noise. "Weekdays are the best times to come here if you want to avoid some of the chaos."

He shelved that piece of information, although it was unlikely he'd have time to repeat this visit anytime soon. To his surprise, he began to enjoy the journey and the details he absorbed, like two women carrying on a conversation from across the street as each manned her stall. No one seemed to mind. He smiled. If they didn't mind people overhearing their conversation, he supposed that was what mattered. Though he didn't understand their words, he could connect with the joyful expressions and their laughter.

Within a few minutes, he'd worked up a sweat, both from walking and the heat of the noonday sun.

"Do you come here often?" he asked.

"I come to shop once a month, because you get wholesale prices for most things."

Practical.

Soon they were walking through an area with rows of stalls, displaying everything from fabric to fresh vegetables to spices to fresh fish and other provisions.

"This is the open market," Naaki said as her grip became firmer.

He was surprised to observe how orderly the open market was. There were clear paths for buyers to walk, though with many stopping by stalls to make purchases, it was a tight squeeze. Market women called out, beckoning them to their merchandise. Naaki shook her head each time, and he followed her example.

They passed a woman selling live snails, sending an uncomfortable shiver up his spine. He supposed escargot was a delicacy here too. He noticed how Naaki walked as far from the snails as possible, but he didn't comment. Next, they passed a basket full of live crabs. Boy was he glad his job didn't require cooking those.

They stopped a few minutes later at a store to buy some bottled water. The store owner was kind enough to offer them chairs to sit. His first instinct had been to turn the offer down, but as he noticed the sweat glistening her face and beading on her upper lip, he followed her example and sat.

After taking a long sip of water, he felt his body begin to cool down though sweat continued dripping down his torso. Naaki took out a handkerchief and blotted her face and arms. Since he'd had no idea he could sweat this much outside the gym, he hadn't carried a handkerchief.

"I have an extra hanky," she offered, dipping into her bag for it.

He smiled. She must have known he wouldn't have one. Either that or she had a natural tendency to nurture. Like the way his mother kept disinfectant wipes and moisturizer in her car. Whatever the case, it made him yearn for the type of closeness with a woman he'd once wished for—the kind that came with a home and children. What he'd thought Arlene could offer him until she'd taught him how misguided such wants were.

"You don't like snails?" he asked, more to keep his mind off the many things he liked about the woman sitting beside him—like her scent, which was so potent in her handkerchief.

She looked surprised before her expression returned to something more even. "I don't like live ones. How did you know?"

"You moved away from them in the market."

She gave him an embarrassed smile. "It gives me an uncomfortable feeling to see them crawl. Crabs, too."

"So you don't eat them?"

She fell silent for a moment. A look crossed her face as though she was trying to decide whether she wanted to answer his question.

"Do you know how crabs are cooked?" Without waiting for a response she continued, "They are placed live in a cooking pot with water and boiled. It's a slow death. Once I knew that, I couldn't eat them anymore."

He didn't know that, and he cringed inside at the image of crabs trying to climb out of boiling water before they inevitably succumbed to their fate. Sensing there was more, he remained quiet.

"At least snails have a quick death. You stick a sharp object into the shell and pop them out." Her lips twitched sadly. "I'm not a vegetarian, so maybe I shouldn't care, but it seems the least we should do is make it as quick and painless as possible. Does that sound hypocritical?"

"It sounds compassionate." He couldn't help taking her hand. "I eat meat too, and I agree with you."

Her intense brown gaze softened with gratitude and something else far more complicated to put in words. He felt a crack in the wall he'd spent the past year building around his heart.

A sudden movement across the street drew their attention. A woman walked by, balancing a big pan on her head. With one hand she dragged along a child who couldn't have been more than four or five, leaving the other free.

"How does she do that?" He pointed at the woman.

"You mean carry something on her head without holding it?" She shrugged. "How do people at the circus walk on high wires?"

It was natural to expect amazing things at the circus, not on any old Saturday on the side of a road. He laughed, shaking his head at the analogy. "Practice?"

"She's probably been doing it for years now. I suppose she discovered there were more important things to do with her hands, like hold her child."

Just then, something quite magical happened. An older man walking toward the woman began to dance as the music coming from the next shop changed to some local and, apparently popular, tune, judging by the way several people whooped. The woman now clutched the pan on her head with her free hand and met him with a very graceful form of the same dance. Moving on from her, the man repeated this with two more women who graciously partnered him for a few steps before going on.

Thane stared in amazement at the unfolding scene. He now understood why African-Americans were so much into music, claiming hip-hop was a way of life. It wasn't a need to be different, but an inherent trait from their roots.

He glanced at Naaki and noticed the pure joy in her eyes as she, along with others laughed and clapped. Turning to him, she said, "Both the music and the dance are called highlife."

"It's beautiful." For some reason it felt like inadequate praise for what he'd just witnessed. "I see what you meant when you said the real culture was with the people."

"Do you want to check out the art center now?"

"Yes."

Buying two extra bottles of water for the road, they continued their journey.

The art center was a large park with sheds where people sold wood carvings, printed cloth, beads, native sandals and an assortment of other crafts. They stopped by a number of tables to look at the displayed items. A necklace made out of sea shells caught his attention on one table and he stopped to look at it.

"Stay here. I'll be right back," Naaki said and disappeared for a few minutes.

While she was away, Thane picked up the necklace. He could just picture it on her— ivory shells against her honey skin. Without hesitation, he asked for the price and paid for it.

She returned, wearing a broad-brimmed straw hat. Beaming, she thrust another towards him.

"I don't think the dark glasses are enough," she said simply.

Smiling, he took it from her. Definitely the nurturing type. If his mother knew he was hanging out with a woman like Naaki, she'd already be planning a wedding. He tried not to tempt himself with wishful thoughts. He wasn't in any position to offer marriage to anyone—especially to Naaki who deserved so much more than he could give.

By the time they returned to her car, it was almost three in the afternoon. Thane felt invigorated, his mind buzzing with the activities of the day.

"Next stop, food," Naaki announced. "I'm hungry."

They hadn't eaten since their separate breakfasts and some bananas they'd bought after their stopover at the art center. It was definitely time to fill their empty stomachs.

# CHAPTER 9

Naaki drove Thane back to her house, since he had left his car there. By the time they arrived, was a little after four. Easing her feet off the clutch and brake pedals, she shifted into neutral and turned off the engine. She glanced over at Thane, unable to resist the urge to gaze at him. Pleasure suffused her every pore, pleasure at sharing a bit of her city with him.

He'd been surprisingly awed by the chaos in the city center. Going in, she'd expected him to be appalled by the brouhaha and insist on being taken back to a less rowdy part of town. She should have known he was tough. He wouldn't back down from a challenge—especially when it meant letting someone down. All right, she conceded, she didn't know the second part for sure, but she had a feeling. A good feeling.

Showing him around had given her a new appreciation for the beauty surrounding her. There were so many things she realized she took for granted, and seeing them through his eyes was unexpectedly wonderful. She didn't want the feeling to end.

"Do you want to come in?" Before he had a chance to respond, she added, "It's tea time and I'm going to brew some herbal tea."

"Tea, huh? Well, this is my cultural awakening day, so I'll bite," he said, flashing an altogether too sexy smile.

A moment later, she unlocked the main door to her bungalow, stepped in, and held it open for Thane. "Welcome to my house."

Her one-bedroom abode was already small and appeared to shrink further when he stepped in. It occurred to her he was only the second man to be alone with her within the walls of her house. The only other, her ex-boyfriend, hadn't stayed more than a few minutes at a time since he didn't like the place. He'd claimed it was too small.

She led Thane to the area doubling as a living and dining room and offered to put away his straw hat. She watched him as he looked around at her simple, yet elegant—in her opinion—décor. She'd gone for comfort and understated class with the furnishing and rug in the living area. The same theme ran through the whole house with little variations for the kitchen and her bedroom, her two favorite rooms. When he didn't say anything for a while, she wondered what he was thinking.

Finally, he turned to face her. "In the US, it is the norm to offer a tour to first-time visitors."

"Really? Why?"

"I don't know. Maybe it's a way to make guests feel at home." The initial frown he gave her disappeared as he grinned. "Imagine how much easier it is to know where the bathroom is."

She laughed. Ordinarily, she might have been embarrassed at such casual conversation, but when her face didn't warm up, she knew she was comfortable around him.

"I'm not inviting myself, of course, so don't—"

"No," she said, surprised herself. Crazy as it sounded, she wanted to. "I'd be happy to give you a tour. Since you've been immersed in Ghanaian culture today, it's only fair that you do something familiar."

Hold on. Had she just invited him to explore her home? Including her bedroom? What had come over her? Was this considered flirting? Probably not. She didn't know how to flirt and decided not to belabor the point. It was an American tradition, so she could take it as a cultural lesson. It wasn't a big deal.

Except, it actually was. Or her heart wouldn't be racing, and her body wouldn't be prickling with awareness.

"In that case, I'm honored."

After a moment's hesitation, she took the plunge. "Let's start in the kitchen. I'll put on the tea before we look at the rest of the house." She led the way. "You have two options: lemongrass, or chamomile with cloves and ginger."

He made a face. "No mixes."

Once again, she found herself intrigued and amused at his protectiveness over his stomach. She shrugged. "My favorite is lemongrass, anyway, although the chamomile is a close second."

While he busied himself with looking around, she stuffed some fresh leaves into a kettle, filled it halfway with water and put it on the stove.

"It's cozy in here," Thane commented "Just like the living room."

"It's my second favorite room in the house," she explained. "I like cooking, so I wanted my kitchen to be comfortable."

She noticed he'd finished his exploration and was now watching her with rapt attention. Folding his arms, he leaned his hip against the countertop. He wasn't too close, but was close enough to make her tingle all over.

Shifting her focus from him and the effect he had on her, she took out a jar of honey, saying, "My father owns a bee farm, so I use honey instead of sugar." When he didn't answer, she ventured a glance and the intensity of his gaze nearly had her in a puddle. "Do you want to see the rest of the house?"

He nodded, pushing away from his support and followed her through the living and dining area to a patio on one side of the house. The polished bamboo furniture was padded with comfortable cushions, wrapped in colorful print cases.

"There's a small vegetable garden in the back." She pointed in the general direction, but didn't offer to show him. She wasn't about to let him see her towel and other way-too-personal items on the clothes line. "That's where the lemongrass came from."

Back inside, she showed him a small storage room and the bathroom, which had two doors, one leading from the living and an adjacent one connecting to her room.

*Not a big deal. Not a big deal.* Her mind chorused those words as they finally reached the door to her bedroom. Turning to him, she tried to smile, but only managed to make the corners of her lips twitch. Concentrating on getting the tour over with, she eased the door open.

"Bedroom." Thane's raspy voice, as he entered, sent a shiver slicing through her. "So is this your favorite room?"

She should have known that comment would come back to taunt her. "Yes," she said, keeping at least an arm's length between them. "How did you know?"

"It's the last room in the house, and you didn't mention anything about any of the others." He shrugged nonchalantly. "Plus I like it."

A sudden thrill invaded her chest. The sense of intimacy about having him in her room, with the new knowledge he had about her attachment to the space, was nearly unbearable. This was her sanctuary, a place she hadn't been comfortable sharing with anyone other than her family and her best friend.

She moved further away from him, sensing how dangerous it would be if he kissed her now, knowing she would let him if he tried. She'd even allow him to lay her on the well-laid bed so they could rumple the sheets together. Fortunately, she seemed to be the only one with an overactive imagination, because his interest was firmly on studying the large painting of Boti Falls on the wall above her double bed.

She averted her eyes in a bid to douse the fire beginning to burn in the pit of her abdomen. It didn't help. Not looking at him, yet knowing he was still there, spun the wheels of her imagination, taking her mind to places she herself had never been—places she shouldn't be thinking about.

"You have your mother's smile." His voice brought her focus back to him. He was holding up a family photo, which usually stood on her nightstand.

She smiled. "Everyone says so."

He turned his gaze on her. "It's a beautiful smile."

Her voice caught when she tried to say "thank you." His gray eyes, zoning in on hers, appeared darker, like granite. Much as she wanted to, she couldn't produce the "beautiful" smile.

The air between them sizzled and the distance seemed to vanish.

Suddenly—thankfully—a sharp whistling pierced the tension, causing her to jump. *The tea.*

"Tea's ready. That's the kettle." She gave herself a mental kick in the head. Of course, he knew what it was. Taking advantage of his diverted attention as he replaced the picture frame, she rushed out.

Moments later, as she poured the fresh brew into mugs, she tried to keep her hands from trembling. He'd assumed that sexy hip-against-the-countertop pose again. Maybe inviting him in wasn't such an inspired idea after all.

"Honey?" she asked, realizing too late how much it sounded like an endearment.

"No, thanks."

Handing him one mug, she scooped two teaspoonfuls of honey into hers and added a squirt of lime juice. She took a sip and closed her eyes with a soft moan as the hot brew soothed her insides. Opening her eyes again, she watched Thane sip his, swishing it in his mouth as though he was tasting wine. A frown knitted his brows. Her heart took a dip when he set aside the mug. She had hoped he would like it, too. Apparently not. She was going to say something when he turned his gaze on her, and her words died instantly.

"I have something for you."

A nervous thrill skittered through her, setting her blood on fire. "What?"

He slipped a hand into his jean pocket and brought out a necklace made from a combination of beads and seashells, polished to a slight shine without destroying their natural essence. Simple and unpretentious. Qualities she found attractive. Why did she have a feeling she'd moved way past the necklace to the man standing in front of her?

"You like it?"

As if he had to ask. The mere fact that he'd thought of getting her something, had the corners of her eyes twitching suspiciously. She nodded, not trusting herself to speak.

"When I spotted it, I wanted to see it on you." He held it up. "May I?"

Nodding again, she placed her mug on the countertop and turned around, sweeping her hair up. As he fastened the necklace around her neck, his fingers brushed against her skin. She trembled. Thankfully he was done before her knees became too weak to support her. When she faced him again, the intensity of his stare robbed her of words.

"Beautiful," he said, his voice a deep rumble.

In reflex, her hand rose to feel the adornment now gracing her neck. She smiled. "Thank you."

"I wasn't talking about the necklace."

She opened her mouth to speak, but her mind seemed to have gone blank.

A soft laugh escaped from him before his gaze dropped to her lips. She knew he was going to kiss her. Her chest tightened, making it hard to breathe, and she gasped as he pulled her into his arms.

When his lips found hers, whatever she was going to say turned into a moan. His warm tongue delved between her parted lips and mated with hers in gentle, yet powerful strokes, creating a symphony in her mouth. The only thing she wanted to say was his name. How could something that felt so good be bad? She melted into him wanting to curl her toes and sigh happily.

It took all her willpower not to whimper when he pulled away.

"So that's what it was."

*Huh?*

"Lemongrass," he said. "The taste I couldn't quite make out before."

He *had* thought about the kiss! And now his voice was low and deep, laden with hunger. At least she wasn't the only one whose emotions were running haywire. The thought surprised, pleased, and scared her all at the same. But the joy dominated, bringing unbidden tenderness to her heart, and she tucked the feeling deep within her. Rather than analyze any of it, she chose to enjoy the simple pleasure of being in his arms.

But it didn't last long. A knock sounded on her front door, startling both on them out of the moment.

"Expecting someone?"

She frowned. "No."

There was no way of telling what the kiss would have led to. She didn't know whether she was even ready to contemplate anything more than a kiss. She should have been grateful for the intervention, but it was with mounting disappointment that she pulled out of his arms as the impatient knocking continued.

❧❧❧

Thane shut his eyes, falling back against the kitchen counter as he tried to bring his body under control. He'd only sought confirmation—satisfaction of curiosity—not to unleash the beast in him. He should have known better than venture another kiss. Now he was paying for it with more than a hard on. *Shit!* He felt like his chest had been blown wide open and his heart was on display. Because now that he'd tasted her sweet lips again, he wanted more. Much more.

Even as he took another sip of tea, intended to have a calming effect, the hot beverage served only to remind him of the taste of citronella on her tongue. Shaking himself, he grabbed her mug. The arrival of a visitor gave him the perfect excuse to leave.

He stepped out of the kitchen in time to catch a glimpse of Naaki's guest, a man, breezing past her into the living area. Almost against his will, Thane suddenly decided leaving was a bad idea. He walked into the living area as the man spoke three words to Naaki.

"Call your mother."

Thane stopped in his tracks, wondering whether he was walking in on a private conversation. There was a definite sense of entitlement in the way the guy regarded Naaki, the way he spoke. *Boyfriend*?

"Is she all right?" The worry in Naaki's voice was unmistakable.

"She said you haven't called in a week."

Thane's grip on the mug tightened as jealousy seized him. Who the hell was this guy who could waltz into her house and speak to her like he had some unique authority to do so?

Glancing over at Naaki, he was surprised at what he observed. He hadn't known her for long, but he already recognized some of her mannerisms. Like the firmly pressed-together lips, the stiff back and the squared shoulders. This wasn't a welcome guest.

Buoyed by his observation, he cleared his throat, causing both of them to look his way. The other guy, who appeared to be about the same height as him—maybe an inch shorter—did a double-take when their eyes met.

His look was hard and hostile. It reeked of jealous boyfriend.

Ignoring him, Thane turned to Naaki. He wanted to ask if she was all right, but he checked himself, refusing to give in to the protectiveness that had gripped him. "I brought you your tea."

She didn't smile, but her eyes softened and her shoulders relaxed slightly. "Thank you." There was a pause before she added his name.

Since she'd turned towards him, Thane took a couple of steps to meet her halfway. As he handed her the mug, their hands brushed, igniting electricity that seared their fingers. All his earlier efforts at calming his body immediately became futile. He was on edge again. Her eyes darted up to meet his and he was trapped in the force of her gaze. For a second, they were the only two people in the world until she turned around and broke contact, bringing him crashing back to reality.

As she walked back towards her guest, Thane lifted his eyes to meet the hostile pair again, fighting with an uncharacteristic desire to gloat. The guy would have to be dense if he didn't notice the "moment" between him and Naaki.

"Who is this?" Mr. Hostile demanded.

The need to gloat turned to fierce dislike at the arrogant scowl on the guy's face.

"This is Thane Aleksander," Naaki said and for her sake, Thane called up all the willpower he could muster to keep his fist from rearranging the bastard's face. "Thane, meet Gyamfi."

Thane offered a hand. "Good to meet you." The lie of the century.

"Likewise." Gyamfi's tone dripped with scorn as he met him with an iron-grip handshake. The dislike was mutual. "Aleksander? You're the executive from America working with MIA."

Thane nodded. At least the guy had his facts straight. "That would be me."

Turning his attention back to Naaki, Gyamfi spoke in Akan. Whatever it was shocked her to the extent of causing her jaw to drop. When she responded, also in Akan, her voice was clipped and low.

A couple more exchanges followed, and each new thing Gyamfi said seemed to have an increasingly upsetting effect. Feeling like an outsider, Thane wondered what was being said. His hands had formed fists as he resisted the urge to deck Gyamfi who couldn't have been saying anything good from the looks of it. Luckily, the need was eliminated when Naaki pointed towards the door.

"Get out," she told Gyamfi.

He sneered, turning a cold eye on Thane before stomping out.

A few moments later, the front door slammed shut and Naaki sank onto one of the chairs.

Worry, now a familiar feeling where she was concerned, made him rush to comfort her. "Are you all right?"

"I think you'd better leave too," she said in a slow measured voice.

At her words, a torrent of anger and shock smacked him in the chest. There was only one reason why she'd be kicking him out. "What did he say?"

The only response he got was silence and tears. Even though every instinct begged him to hold her, he didn't move an inch, preferring to hold on to the anger. He had a gut feeling it would insulate him against whatever she was about to say.

Her chin trembled as she spoke. "He thinks you and I are...lovers."

Thane bit back a curse. Now he definitely regretted not giving in and breaking Gyamfi's nose when he had the chance. "Who the hell is he?"

Lifting deeply distressed eyes, she said, "We used to date."

*Used to.* Thane's mind latched on to those two words. The guy was supposed to be out of the picture, so what did he care who the hell she slept with?

"He said it's why I got hired. He never believed I was cut out for the corporate world." Her voice shook, but she held herself together even as the tears traced their way down her cheeks. "He always said I'm too kind and caring; a good wife and mother, but—"

Thane swore. It was guys like that who gave men a bad name. He came to squat beside her, taking both her hands in his. "Believe me, Naaki, any man would be lucky to have you in his bed, but that's not why we hired you. Mr. Boateng and I thoroughly assessed each applicant and you came up tops."

She smiled gratefully. His heart clenched. He didn't want her gratitude. He wanted to pull her back into his arms, but knew it would be the worst thing he could possibly

175

do at this moment. A second later, the option was taken away as she withdrew her hands from his grip. Using the back of her hand, she dried her tears.

"Naaki." He had so much to say, but he decided only one was important. "If that man told you you're only good for the home, either he gets off on putting you down or he really doesn't know you."

Thane had a hard time believing it would be the second option, because even in the little time he'd known her, there was no doubt in his mind what an intelligent woman she was. She had plenty to offer in the corporate world, and yes, in the home—if she so decided. "If he's not man enough to believe in you, then he doesn't deserve you." And good riddance was all he could think.

She took in a deep breath and let it out with a sigh, although she didn't look convinced.

"Are you forgetting about your presentation yesterday? Those were four executives who are only concerned about their bottom line and you blew them away." He tried to capture her gaze. "That was all you."

Finally, she nodded, but her eyes hardened. He knew what was coming even before she spoke.

"You should go."

# CHAPTER 10

Naaki's heart skipped a beat when Thane's voice filtered through the open door. She shut her eyes, absorbing his sweet baritone, as his laughter reached her ears. Pain slashed her resolve and hitched her breath. When she'd asked him to leave on Saturday, she'd fully expected to emerge unscathed. She hadn't counted on feeling so...alone. In the privacy of her thoughts, the memory of his kisses haunted her. His taste would slip over her tongue at the oddest times and make her lightheaded.

It was a good thing she hadn't seen much of him these past four days—five, if you counted Sunday. Thankfully, her time with him had ended and she'd been in the Account Management Department this week.

She'd absorbed a wealth of information from working with her new "buddies" and had attended several client meetings. If she hadn't gone home exhausted every night, she didn't know how she would have survived this long.

It perplexed her how much she missed working alongside him. While she was learning a lot from the AEs, working with them wasn't half as invigorating as working with Thane had been. She hadn't expected to miss him. Then again, when it came to Thane, many things were unexpected. Like his willingness to brainstorm on ideas rather than impose his own on someone else. He appreciated the fact that the business environment here was different from any he'd encountered before and was willing to learn—and with enthusiasm, no less.

When his opinion differed from the team's, he had a way of putting his points across in an objective way, allowing them to develop strategies everyone believed in and supported. She'd also discovered that some things in business were the same no matter where you were located—things like the fact that a motivated workforce tended to be more productive than an unmotivated one.

The talent to inspire seemed to come naturally to Thane. In the time Naaki had been at MIA, it had become obvious everyone liked him, though she had a suspicion none of them liked him quite the way she did. His presence had also injected some confidence into the clients' view of the agency, and prospects for new business were looking up.

The most unexpected thing, though, was how she reacted to him. Like right now, although she couldn't discern what he was saying, just hearing the sound of his voice bathed her skin in goose bumps. Rubbing her arms, she tried to push his voice out of her head and force her attention back to the computer monitor. How else was she going to complete the document she was supposed to be writing or prove that Gyamfi was completely wrong about her?

Just as she saved the final changes on her report, Kevin, one of the AE's she'd already buddied with this week, walked to the desk next to hers.

Shaking his head, he commented to no one in particular, "Thane is on point, people. I was just discussing my client's new brief with him and just like that—" He snapped his fingers. "—he came up with some great input. It's like the man's mind is always spinning."

A lump formed in Naaki's throat as someone else responded with another comment praising the man. She wished they would choose some other time for this conversation—preferably one when she wasn't in attendance.

"By the way, Naaki, he wants to see you," Kevin said.

She took in a sharp breath, realizing she'd been holding it while they talked about him. A mixture of joy and anxiety dampened her palms as she thanked Kevin and stood.

Though she tried to push aside her confused emotions, the sight of him through his open office door made her efforts futile.

Afforded this private moment to observe him without his knowledge, she paused. He was hunched over, scrutinizing something on his laptop—a position that was definitely bad for his back. She chewed on her lower lip. He looked gorgeous with his thick black eyebrows almost touching and his lips pursed in a most sexy way. He wore a striped shirt without a tie and his sleeves were folded up to his elbows, revealing strong arms with a light film of hair. It made her think of his chest hair—well, the little she'd seen when he'd had a button undone.

When he lifted his hands to smooth out his hair—not that the effort was needed—she was reminded she still hadn't gotten the chance to run her fingers through it. Shaking off an onslaught of sensations, she stepped forward and knocked even though the door was open.

His head shot up and the frown immediately disappeared, leaving only his formidable good looks.

"Naaki," he said. "Good. I wanted to see you."

It was utterly ludicrous that his words should generate any positive emotion whatsoever, yet an inexplicable happiness had her floating. He wanted to see her. From the warmth now creeping from her chest down to her core, it seemed as if she'd waited all week for this moment.

"Here I am."

He smiled, motioning for her to sit down. Shutting the door behind her, she eased herself onto a seat, returning his smile with one of her own, and waited. Although he gave no indication he'd missed her, she couldn't help thinking about their kisses, and her eyes briefly dropped to his lips. What was happening to her? She'd never been the type of woman whose thoughts wandered—and certainly not to such sensuous destinations.

"It's Thursday. You're supposed to report your progress to me before the end of each week."

"Oh, yes." She hoped her response didn't sound like she'd forgotten—she hadn't—or that her mind had been on *other* things just now—which it had. *Ei!* She needed to work harder at concentrating on work rather than how good it felt to be in the same room with him. She'd never felt this way about anyone. No man had ever wielded the kind of power to make her yearn for him with a force that rivaled—no, *threatened*—her focus on career ambitions.

Luckily she'd had enough presence of mind to carry her thumb drive with her. At least some part of her brain was still functioning. She could only thank God for such small mercies. Taking a deep, calming breath, she handed it to him.

"You should sit up," she said and almost cringed when his eyes narrowed. She had to admit, it came out bossier than intended.

Feeling a need to explain, she added, "Crouching isn't good for your back."

Without answering, he plugged her thumb drive into his computer, but his posture improved. He beckoned. "Pull up your chair."

She winced at the curt command and wondered if it was his way of punishing her for her officious statement. She did as she was told, fighting the urge to lean in for a closer whiff of his musky scent.

They went over her report then discussed her impressions of her first two weeks at the agency. After that, they reviewed her internship schedule, making adjustments wherever necessary.

Twenty minutes later, Thane saved the document and returned her disk. It couldn't have been soon enough for her. Glad for the opportunity to put some distance between them, she started wheeling herself back to her original position, placing his desk between them. It wasn't to be, however. Thane grabbed the arm of her chair in one quick motion, halting her progress.

"Where are you going?"

Her gaze shot up and collided with his. Many things went through her mind—like how difficult breathing had suddenly become. "I want to show you something."

Was he planning to kiss her? Her mind danced around several options of things he could show her; none of them appropriate for the office. She stopped breathing entirely as thrilling sensations congregated in her lower abdomen, travelling south.

"I'm moving out of the hotel," he announced, diverting his attention to the computer. "Admin gave me a few options, and I narrowed them down to three. I'd like your opinion."

"Okay," she said, surprised she'd managed to respond without closing her eyes and moaning. Returning to her place beside him, she redirected her attention to the monitor.

The first picture was of a two bedroom bungalow in the Airport Residential area. It had a small yard made mostly of concrete with only a tiny patch of grass. He clicked on the next image to show 3D photos of the insides. It looked neat, but she wasn't drawn to it in any special way.

"It's in a good neighborhood, but I don't like the yard," she said.

He made a face. "Me neither."

As he spoke, he clicked again to show the second option, also in the Airport Residential area. Though a healthy-looking lawn and flowers surrounded the house, the interior didn't appear to be much of an improvement over the first. She was about to comment when he placed his hand on hers. The casual gesture silenced her.

"Don't say anything yet. Look at the third one and then consider all three together."

She nodded, studying the photos of a three-bedroom house in East Cantonments. The yard was smaller than the previous ones, although the lawn was well-groomed and had a more harmonious arrangement of flowers. The interior showed bare white walls with polished-wood ceilings and tiled floors. The inset closets were similar to the first two, but it was the kitchen that sold her. The bold olive green walls contrasted well with the neutral hues of the floors and the maple cabinets. Though it stood out from the rest of the house, another photo revealed a section of the corridor with part of the kitchen, showing its complementary effect.

"You like this one." His voice, echoing the same approval as she felt, caressed her senses.

"I do." Without thinking, she added, "I can imagine cooking in there."

He gave her arm a gentle squeeze. "Consider yourself invited, whenever you wish."

Cooking for Thane. Why did the idea hold so much appeal? She became newly aware of his hand on her arm as her skin heated beneath it.

Raising her eyes back to his, she saw a different sort of invitation. Was her mind playing tricks on her or could Thane be battling with some of the same emotions she was fighting? Or was she deluding herself? As heat crept up her neck and face, whatever she thought she saw disappeared.

ᘓᔓᘓᔓ

Thane stared. "No way. Did you just blush?"

He took a closer look. The evidence was right there. The crimson hue returned briefly. Stunned, he realized he'd never really considered the possibility of a dark-skinned person blushing with color.

He was tempted to laugh when she straightened her already pristine posture and turned up her nose in a queenly fashion. "I don't blush."

Even as she contested the possibility, another wave of color tinged her cheeks. Now that he'd noticed, he was amazed he hadn't seen it before. She was a blusher! "I know what I saw."

"It's not possible," she persisted weakly. "One of the many benefits of African skin is its ability to conceal a person's innermost emotions."

*Innermost emotions.* He groaned inwardly. Now, why would she go and use an expression that gave him all sorts of ideas? As if her nearness the past half hour weren't enough to stir up some deep emotions of his own.

It wasn't just one thing. It was the way she smiled when she approved and frowned when she didn't, the way she walked, the way she came up with ideas—naturally—as if she hadn't needed to think about them. Even her sometimes cautious nature, an attribute he'd never specifically admired in a woman, was endearing. He never knew when he was going to do or say something to earn her smile or disapproval. But that just made every moment spent with her all the more exciting.

Discovering she was a blusher, only served to fuel the raging need he'd been trying to keep under lock and key. He fought the temptation to provoke more of the charming, crimson blush. Was the list of things he found attractive about her ever going to be exhausted?

He touched her face, and his heart shuddered. It felt good to cup her cheek. Her soft, smooth skin radiated warmth, which confirmed what she was denying.

"Sweetheart, that's like saying I can't recognize a tomato when I'm wearing shades." It amazed him how he got the words out without his voice cracking in the process.

Her comeback died away as she conceded—grudgingly, he could tell—the logic in his argument. Her lips settled into a delightful little pout. He threw his head back and laughed. *God, I love her.*

Stunned at the thought, he sobered but couldn't deny the conviction in the words. Luckily, his office phone rang, saving him from the need to analyze his stupidity. But even as he picked up the call, he knew at the back of his mind he'd just stepped over to the point of no return. In five and a half months, when the time came to return home, he'd be crushed. He could only hope he hadn't put her in the same predicament.

☙❧☙

The past twenty-four hours had been torturous for Thane. Despite his best efforts to disregard his feelings for Naaki, his heart opposed him at every turn. After their meeting yesterday, he'd steered clear of her. But now that he was standing in front of the entire team in MIA's large conference room, avoidance was impossible.

He was about to address the team in the first of several meetings to acquaint MIA staff with Black & Black. The goal was to develop a hybrid culture that took the best of what both agencies had to offer. It also meant he was about to reveal some details on the nature of the relationship between the two agencies.

All eyes were on him, but he was aware only of Naaki. He wondered how she would react to the information he was about to disclose. Though some members of staff looked excited, others seemed wary. No one had touched the tea and coffee provided.

"I want to start by saying thank you for the making me feel welcome to Ghana and to MIA," he began, deciding to get right to the point. "My purpose in coming here was to facilitate the merger between our two agencies. I realize this is going to be a big adjustment for all of us, but I trust we'll emerge from this a better company."

His laptop was hooked up to the projector, and he opened a document that immediately projected onto the white wall. "I'll start by talking to you about Black & Black and how we are planning for this partnership to work. We'll also have the opportunity to hear from our CEO, Steven Black."

He went through the history of the company that started as Black & Son, a small print shop owned by Anthony Black and his son, Steven. He'd been in his mid-thirties when he started the company. He wasn't one of those geniuses who quit school to build multi-million dollar companies. He'd paid his dues, going to four years of college and two years of graduate school, and he'd started small, approaching business with caution and diligence. He was honest with his customers, focused on building relationships rather than the bottom-line.

The company had remained relatively small, relying mainly on word of mouth as its own source of advertising until Anthony Black's death fifteen years ago. His younger son, Leo, who had just finished business school, joined the company, and the brothers changed the name to Black & Black. With Steven as the new CEO, the agency adopted a more aggressive approach to recruiting clients.

Today, they were one of the largest advertising firms on the East Coast with a significant presence in Europe and Asia, and now Africa, through affiliations.

Thane paused for questions.

There were none, so he went on to discuss some specifics on fusing the two agencies' cultures, although it sounded like MIA would be doing more adapting than Black & Black. The plan was to bring some stability to the local agency and make available some of Black & Black's patented processes to MIA, while allowing the local agency to function as an independent affiliate.

It was clearly an unequal merger and some of the faces looking back at him didn't appear pleased. He was used to such looks, though. It happened in every company going through restructuring. People didn't like change. Himself included.

Although the changes that applied to him had nothing to do with business and everything to do with Naaki. He had to get used to his heart working overtime whenever she was near, and the desire to involve her in decisions troubled him. He told himself it was because he was in a new country—her country. Truth be told, it just felt good when she approved.

After thirty minutes, he gave them a short break and when they returned, he Skyped in Steven Black who gave one of his CEO motivational speeches.

Thane was listening until Naaki shifted in her chair. His attention was drawn to her even though he'd been completely aware of her all through his spiel. She touched her face lightly before crossing her arms, a gesture that gently pressed her breasts up to show more cleavage—unintentionally, he suspected. He suddenly felt hot and had a hard time concentrating.

A few minutes into Steve's dialogue, she pursed her lips briefly. Little gestures he shouldn't even have noticed, but how could he not when every simple, natural thing she did seemed so damned erotic? He could only think of how much he wanted to end this meeting, whisk her to his hotel room, and make love to her.

Off limits, he told himself as if that would help. He was in love with her, but because he couldn't do a thing about it, it felt like a prison sentence. What he needed to worry about was serving his time without exposing his feelings for her—a difficult task, considering he couldn't take his eyes off her.

When Steve said goodbye to them, Thane was ready to leave the room. However, they still had to wrap things up. Taking another few minutes, they discussed aspects of MIA's processes and culture that the staff absolutely wanted to keep. After giving each person until Monday to come up with a list of the top three changes they wanted to see, he made his escape.

He'd barely been in his office five minutes when she knocked. He bit back a curse. Obviously some recalcitrant angel had it in for him.

"Come in."

She took a few steps in, her eyes radiant. She folded her arms and smiled. He would have given anything to hold her, but he remained seated at his desk as if that position would offer him some kind of protection. Actually, it did prevent her from witnessing the physical evidence of what her presence did to him.

"So it's really happening," she said. "There's no going back now."

He only nodded, because work was the farthest thing from his mind when she looked so enticing, so unaware of the images going through his mind.

"I'm glad you're here. It's good for MIA," she said. "I—uh emailed a memo to you and Mr. Boateng this morning. I was wondering if you'd had a chance to look at it."

His mind went to her email, which asked for four days off next week to write exams.

"Yes, I did." Scrolling quickly through his inbox, he found her mail and opened the attachment. He printed a copy and appended his signature on it. "Just leave a copy with Admin."

"Thank you," she said, receiving the paper.

He didn't take his eyes off her when she turned around to leave. As she shut the door on her way out, their eyes met and she paused. It would be another week before he saw her again. "Good luck, Naaki."

She thanked him again and closed the door.

# CHAPTER 11

*T*hank *God it's Friday.* The words hadn't stopped repeating themselves in Naaki's head since she woke up. Not only had she completed her exams, but based on her assessment, she expected to do well. She was one step closer to becoming a member of the Chartered Institute of Marketing, which would open so many doors for her career-wise.

The significance of today for her, however, lay in the fact that she was going back to work—back to Thane. Mentally, she'd been counting the days even as she prepared for and wrote her papers.

By a quarter to eight she was walking into the reception area where she spent a few minutes chatting with the receptionist. Then under the pretext of saying hello after her four days off, she passed through each office greeting people.

She saved Thane for last, and by the time she reached the door to his office, her excitement threatened to overwhelm her. Her beaming smile died away when she knocked and got no answer. Frowning, she knocked again. The door was ajar, so she pushed it open only to find an empty office. Disappointment reared its ugly head, bursting her bubble.

Mr. Boateng hadn't been in his office either. She assumed they had gone to a meeting. It was just as well. What would she have said, anyway? While she had spent days longing to see him again, there was no reason for him to do the same...not really. Yet a part of her remained optimistic. She'd waited a whole week, what was another couple of hours? Everybody else appeared to be happy to see her, so her expectations couldn't be that far-fetched. Could they?

To her utter frustration, she found herself going through her day in a perfunctory manner, battling to concentrate. Two hours after lunch, he was still not back. She decided to step outside for fresh air. She needed to clear her head and squelch the overpowering need to just see him.

Aku intercepted Naaki on her way out, engaging her in a conversation she wasn't particularly interested in. After a few minutes of listening to a rundown of Aku's problems with her teenage daughter who was home on mid-term vacation, Naaki ventured a question she hoped didn't sound too personal.

"Aku, where's Thane?"

The older woman appeared taken aback only for a moment. "Oh, nobody told you?"

"Told me what?" It had to be something bad, Naaki deduced.

"He stayed at home today. He's not well."

The news hit Naaki like a punch. "Since when? Is he all right?"

"Oh, I'm sure he'll be fine," Aku said with a casual wave of her hand. "It's just malaria."

"Malaria?" Naaki cringed at the alarm in her own voice.

"He's been to the hospital. He should be fine by Monday."

"You don't understand. For him it's not 'just' malaria. This must be his first time getting it." Naaki couldn't imagine how terrible he must be feeling right now. Her desire to see him multiplied. But it wouldn't be possible. She didn't even know whether he'd already moved from the hotel.

"He's a tough man." Aku chuckled. "At least, that's what he said yesterday."

"You've seen him?"

"Of course." Aku rolled her eyes in a fashion that would have put any teenager to shame. "Everyone has."

Except me, Naaki thought. "Is he still at the hotel?"

"No, he moved out,"

"Oh." Her shoulders slumped. Without warning, her eyes prickled with tears—the culmination of her emotions raging wildly all day. She blinked, turning aside. "Thanks."

"I can give you the directions if you want. They're already printed." As Aku handed Naaki a sheet of paper, her eyes widened as though an idea had just occurred to her. She opened her drawer and took out a greeting card. "You can take this with you. Everyone has signed it, except you."

Words eluded Naaki. Was it really okay to go and visit Thane? Alone? Would he appreciate the concern or would it appear as an invasion of privacy? He needed rest—a lot of it. On one hand, she was elated at the prospect of seeing him but worried she might be venturing into the very situation she ought to avoid. The yearning to see Thane overrode her worry, however, and she took the card.

"Grace mentioned something about dropping by today. Maybe you two can go together," Aku added.

"Thanks, Aku."

Naaki's next stop was the media manager's desk.

"Hi, Grace." Once her mind was made up, Naaki had to struggle not to sound too eager. "Aku says you were planning on visiting Thane."

Grace made a face. "Yes, but I can't anymore. My husband and I have a date. The children are with my parents for the weekend. It isn't often that Ebo and I have time to ourselves." Despite her apologetic tone, her look was the complete opposite. "But this is wonderful. You can take this with you." She reached under her desk and pulled out a bag.

"What is it?"

"A healthy goodie bag." Grace smiled. "Fruits."

Naaki opened the bag and frowned at the contents. "These are all local fruits."

Grace held up her hand. "Correction. Medicinal fruits."

"Yes, I know but—" How would she explain knowing about Thane's aversion to trying out new foods? She shook her head. He would have to decide what to do with them. "Fine."

Grace stood and shouted for everyone's attention. "Naaki's going by Thane's place, if you want to give her anything."

"Grace!" Naaki flushed with embarrassment but had no time to think about it. Within minutes, she had a couple more get-well-soon packages in her custody. She grimaced. Now everyone knew she was going there. Worse, she couldn't back out.

"Sorry, dear," Grace said. "It's Friday. Everyone has somewhere else to go. Besides, we've all been there once already."

∽∽∽

Naaki recognized the house as soon as she turned toward it. Armed with the directions Aku had given her, the house was easy to find. He'd chosen the third option she'd seen in the office. She eased the car to a stop in front of the short wall surrounding it.

Staring through the windshield, she exhaled through her mouth. Her hands trembled slightly. The cocktail of mixed emotions whirling in the pit of her stomach made her queasy.

After a while, and several deep breaths, she stepped out of the car, swung her purse over her shoulder, and grabbed the goodie bags from the back seat. Casting a look around the quiet street, she made sure to lock the car before taking her first step towards the house.

A part of her wanted to rush in, while the more cautious side felt like leaving the gifts at his door without him knowing she was ever there. But she couldn't do either. She wanted—needed—to see him. Setting eyes on him was something she simply had to do. She believed this with a certainty she couldn't understand. She wouldn't stay long, she decided, just long enough to confirm he was all right.

The wrought iron gate was open, so she stepped inside. The reality of the exterior was more striking than the picture. Even the lawn looked incredibly healthy for early-

September when the city received only residual showers from the rainy season. Extending around the main building, the stone-paved walkway was hedged by various flowers. The pathway led to a veranda, which sported a variety of potted plants.

Her focus was, however, not on the manicured surroundings. Not when the man inside the house held so much more appeal.

At the door, she knocked and waited. Noticing that her palms were sweaty, she placed the bags on the floor and wiped her hands on her skirt. Her stomach was in knots and her hands still trembled. She placed her palm over her lower abdomen in a bid to persuade her stomach to settle. She knocked again, fighting the urge to chew on her nails.

At last, she heard the blessed sound of the door unlocking, then the solid mahogany panel swung open, bringing her face-to-face with Thane. She gasped. He stared at her with stricken eyes, his face pallid. His lips, which were usually a rich pink, now looked pale. By contrast, his nose sported a red hue, sorely standing out against his sallow face. His thick black hair and t-shirt were damp with perspiration, both beginning to cling to his skin. He looked ready to pass out.

She never thought someone else's anguish could paralyze her, but at this moment she found herself transfixed.

"Thane." His name tumbled out of her in a pained cry, as though somehow she were responsible for his illness.

"Naaki."

No other words needed to be spoken. She fell into his arms, hugging and being hugged so tightly she could barely breathe. But breathing wasn't her concern at this moment. All she cared about was holding him and absorbing the overwhelming pleasure of being in his arms. He buried his face in the crook of her neck, and she felt the warmth of his breath all the way down to her core. She gave a contended sigh.

He tightened his embrace, and as she pressed her body against his, her stomach came into contact with the rigid evidence of his arousal. Her breath snagged. Instead of feeling awkward, she burned with a desire to explore this new discovery, to embrace him more intimately.

But right now, she needed to think about another kind of heat—the one radiating from his body due to malaria. Reluctantly, she pulled away, worried. "You're hot."

He managed a tired-looking smile, which brightened his eyes significantly. "So are you."

Naaki flushed. If he wasn't unwell, she'd have swatted him for the comment. Instead, she placed the back of her hand against his neck. "You should sit down." Remembering the goodie bags on the veranda, she retrieved them. "These are from people at the office."

He acknowledged her statement with a grunt, stepping aside for her to enter.

The door opened straight into his living room. Like the exterior, the interior was more beautiful than the pictures had portrayed. The simple furniture had a masculine elegance; exactly what she would have expected. The room lacked that lived-in look and gave the feel of a hotel rather than a home. She supposed he hadn't had time to add his personal touches to it.

She took a seat on the couch when he gestured for her to sit. He sat next to her, leaning back and resting his head against the high back of the sofa.

She studied him awhile. "Are you all right?"

He groaned. "I've been better."

"Didn't you take any preventive medication before travelling?"

He scowled. "A lot of things were happening in the couple of weeks leading to my departure and I forgot to start taking them a week prior to my trip like I was supposed to."

How he could forget to take medication was a mystery, but his candidness was strangely appealing. "You've seen a doctor, right?

"Yes, and I've taken my prescription, in case you were wondering." He turned his face toward her. "What's in the bags?"

Sensing he was only trying to divert the conversation from himself, she decided to humor him. She took out the get-well-soon card and handed it to him.

"This is from all of us," she said.

He took the card out of the envelope and opened it. After a while, he turned it over again to look at the picture on the front—a cartoon figure sick in bed with a thermometer in his mouth.

He chuckled softly. "Looks like they got the nose right."

"The rest are fruits from Grace, juice from the account management department and magazines from Creative," Naaki added. "Oh, and Tony from Planning sent the first draft of a research report he's working on."

He nodded, taking the printed report. He flipped through the document once before laying it on the coffee table.

"I can put these away for you," Naaki offered.

He nodded again, and pointed to the kitchen.

It took Naaki just a couple of minutes to find space in the fridge for the fruits. Returning to the living room, she found Thane lying on the couch. The sight filled her with tenderness...and concern. She tested his temperature again. He was burning up. "You need a cold shower."

"Not gonna happen," he murmured. Even in the weak voice, she could detect a touch of humor. "I'm good right here on the couch. What I need is a blanket."

She understood his reluctance to exert any energy in his condition, especially in order to take a shower when he might already be feeling chilly. But it was important to keep his body cool, and lying here wasn't going to achieve that aim. "At least let me towel you down."

He remained quiet, and for a moment Naaki actually considered begging him to let her help him. It was definitely time to leave, she decided. She'd accomplished what she came here to do. So why was she so reluctant to say goodbye?

"What would you need?" Thane eventually asked.

Her mind filled with joy and jettisoned any plans to leave. "I'll need a bowl or bucket and a towel."

"Bowl's in the kitchen." He started to rise up. "I'll get the towel."

She placed her hand on his shoulder to restrain him. "No. I'll get it. Just tell me where it is."

Allowing her the victory, he told her where he kept the linens. Even though she wouldn't call him on it, Naaki had a suspicion he was grateful he didn't have to get up. She hurried to get the towel then filled a bowl with water. She returned to his side, pausing for a moment to watch him. He appeared peaceful, with his eyes shut and one hand resting under his head.

"Thane," she called quietly as she sat by him, "I'm here."

He made a soft sound in response. His eyelids moved, but he didn't open his eyes.

"Are you ready?"

He grunted again.

Naaki wet the towel and squeezed the water out of it. She worked on his handsome face first, hoping some color would return to it.

"Do you have a headache?"

He shook his head. "Not really. Just a...heaviness."

"You need to rest." Wetting the towel again, she applied it to his neck.

He sucked in a sharp breath when the coolness came in contact with his skin, but relaxed again as she continued. Swabbing his entire neck several more times, she moved on to his arms. She checked his temperature again and noted a slight decline. She sighed with relief. A shower would really have been the best, but she didn't have the heart to push the matter. In fact, she had no right to.

"Thane," she said cautiously, hoping she wasn't overstepping her boundaries. He opened his eyes a slice. "I think you need to take off your t-shirt."

To her relief, he raised himself, slid off the garment in one smooth motion and laid back, without a word. The sight of his naked torso, richly covered with a light layer of hair, rendered her speechless. It was more beautiful than she'd imagined. The velvety black hair veiled his chest and tapered down into a thin line running down the middle of his impressive six-pack until it disappeared under the waistband of his pants.

Her arm froze in midair as her eyes riveted on him. She gulped. It appeared she'd bitten off more than she could chew, because *her* body was now on fire. Fighting to focus on the task at hand, she soaked the towel again. But as she cooled him off, the wet hair only made it harder to concentrate. At this rate, she was going to need a shower herself.

After a few minutes, she checked his temperature again. Thankfully, it seemed to have returned to almost normal. His face looked relaxed, his breathing deep and measured. Had he fallen asleep? She turned her hand over, placing her palm on his firm abdomen. In an instant, her world shrank to the space occupied by just the two of them. As though sensing this cosmic shift, Thane opened his eyes.

She was trapped.

"Thank you," he whispered, his voice barely audible, but it was the only thing she could hear.

My pleasure, she wanted to say, but the words simply didn't materialize out of the muddle that was her thoughts. She returned his unwavering stare. Her pulse escalated when he linked his fingers with hers and caressed the back of her hand with his thumb. There was tenderness in his gaze, sheathed by a veil of want—desire she recognized because she was consumed by it, too.

"Is it inappropriate to kiss you?"

She could have said yes, and she knew he'd have accepted it unconditionally. With the one word, she could have saved them any potential regrets and apologies. But in his embrace earlier, she'd felt like her world had been set aright. She needed this kiss more than he could ever imagine—perhaps even more than he did hers.

She shook her head. "Kiss me, Thane."

He sat up quicker than she'd have expected of a sick person. As he closed the gap between them, his eyes never left hers. Inches away from her, he cupped her face. Stroking her features gently, he brushed his lips over hers. Her eyes closed of their own volition, her lips parted in anticipation of his tongue's entry. He was still just a breath away, lingering, taunting, fueling an impatience she never knew she possessed. It was all she could do not to scream.

Unable to take any more of the waiting, she arched her back to push herself forward until the blessed moment when their lips joined. She sucked in a breath as her brain shut down from the pleasure. She moaned, wrapping her arms around him. It was the last thing she did—consciously. After that, the kiss took on a life of its own, carrying them on delicious waves of delight, dying down only when they needed to catch their breaths.

"Is anyone going to miss you?" he whispered against her lips.

*Anyone*? Had the kiss scrambled her mind so much that she couldn't understand a simple question? His gentle caress of her face and the smoldering intensity of his gaze didn't help matters.

Her confusion must have shown on her face, because he added, "If you don't go home today?"

She started to shake her head, but hesitated. Then asked herself why. After all, she had no one. Not since she'd walked away from her last relationship. She didn't want anyone. At least, that's what she'd tried to tell herself. Yet Thane's question had exposed the lie and laid bare her yearning to have someone. *Him.*

# CHAPTER 12

I can't stay."
Three simple words. They shouldn't have caused any pain to utter, yet they sliced through Naaki like daggers. She hoped he hadn't heard the heaviness of barely held back tears in her voice. She wanted nothing more than to stay, to see what happened. That was precisely why she couldn't. He needed all the rest he could get, and with her emotions running wild, there was no telling what she'd want to tempt him to do.

Her body trembled at his touch; hot embers of desire burned her blood, ignited by the palpable hunger in the depths of his stunning gray eyes. She could see the disappointment in them, along with the unasked question. *Why?* Yet he nodded, accepting her decision.

Neither of them made a move to break away. Gradually the space between them shrank to nothing. When he kissed her this time, there was no teasing, no taunting. He was possessive, passionate, and she was lost. A long, drawn-out moan rose from her throat, mirroring a groan from him. When he broke off the kiss, she whimpered as though her air supply had been stolen.

Entwining their fingers again, they both sighed, but neither of them spoke.

Thane was the first to venture a word. "I never expected to meet someone like you."

Naaki couldn't wrap her mind around how incredibly happy she was at this moment, knowing her feelings were reciprocated. "Me neither. You're so..." her voice trailed off as she tried to find the right word.

"Genteel? Dashing?" Thane provided light-heartedly.

She giggled. "I was going to say easygoing."

"That's good too." The corners of his lips curved up. "So you don't think I'm rude anymore?"

A tinge of warmth touched her cheeks. "It was a hasty first impression."

"I'm glad you changed your mind." With a tired sigh, he leaned sideways against the back of the couch. His eyes narrowed with a look of curiosity. "Why do you always tie your hair back?"

Momentarily taken off guard by the question, a frown settled on her brows. She shrugged. "It's easier, I suppose."

"Easier isn't always best." He reached out his arm to the back of her head, and in an instant, the scrunchy in her hair came off. Her curls fell in gentle waves around her face, the ends barely licking her shoulders. "The first time I saw you, I imagined doing exactly this."

She felt as if she'd just been thrust into some new level of familiarity—one in which they shared preferences.

"You have lovely hair," he continued, his baritone almost hypnotizing her as his fingers gently raked through her tresses. "When we're alone, I want to see it."

Naaki swallowed. From the way her heart jumped, he might as well have asked her to strip. Unconsciously, she inched closer to allow him the latitude to play with her hair.

"Tell me about your exams."

She had no idea how she managed to relate the information when her mind was so lost in the spine-tingling sensations flooding her body. Just as she was about to lean in further, his hand dropped and he winced. Immediately, alarm invaded her. "What's wrong?"

"I think I better lie down."

"Oh." Without having to think, her arms moved to assist, helping him settle in a comfortable position. "I should go now, so you can rest properly."

"Okay."

"Will you be all right? Is there anything I can do before leaving?"

"Don't worry about me. I just need to rest like the good doctor told me and take my meds at eight." Taking in a deep breath, he began to rise up again. "I'll walk you out."

"No, it's okay."

"Someone has to lock the door."

Conceding the point, she didn't argue further. He was a grown man after all, and he could take care of himself. Getting on his feet was a cautious process, but he managed it quite well, giving her new appreciation for his bare-chested, six-foot frame.

"Thanks for coming by."

"When you didn't show up at work today, I—" I had a bad day, she wanted to confess. She realized how much she'd come to expect his presence at the office, how much he meant to her. She'd definitely taken the plunge. "I had to see you."

He pressed his lips on the crown of her head. "I'm glad you did."

She shuddered, tempted to wrap her arms around him and relax against his solid chest. Instead, she steeled herself and turned toward the door, afraid any delay would cause her to change her mind.

She led the way as they walked toward the door and weighed the option of passing by tomorrow to check on him instead of calling. When she turned around, intending to ask if he had a preference, she discovered he was no longer right behind her. He'd fallen back and was now holding on to the back of one of the armchairs, his breathing heavy. Then his knees buckled and he crumpled.

In that moment, Naaki knew real fear. "Thane!"

Panicked, she rushed to his side with only one thought on her mind, to intercept him before he hit the floor. Her singular focus heightened her senses, propelling her forward. By the time she reached his side, he was on his knees. Though he still held on to the chair, his grip was slipping. She grabbed him around the waist with trembling arms, barely managing to halt his fall.

She cradled him against her heaving breasts. "Oh my God, Thane."

His eyes appeared spaced out, his breathing fast and shallow. "Naaki." His voice was barely above a whisper, but it was steady.

Relief washed over her when he spoke. "What happened?"

He winced, closing his eyes. "Damn room is spinning."

Guilt replaced relief. She must have caused him to exert more energy than he should have, which would explain the dizzy spell. This was all her fault. What had she been thinking, asking him to kiss her? He needed rest, not passion. And she was going to make sure he got it.

"I need to get you back to the sofa. Can you walk?"

He exhaled heavily. "Yes, I think so."

She hefted his arm onto her shoulder and curled hers around his waist. Slowly, they rose up and made their way back to the couch more steadily than she could have hoped for. Settling him down, she sat by his side, concern pervading her every pore. "How are you feeling?"

He cursed softly. "Like I'm floating."

"I'm so sorry. I shouldn't have let you—"

"Kiss you?" His lips stretched out faintly. "I'd collapse a thousand times to kiss you again."

His words roused all those wicked thoughts in her mind again, even though she wasn't about to let him try.

He must have seen her guilty expression. "Don't worry, I'll be fine."

He was probably right. Dizziness was normal with malaria. But she was concerned, so just to be sure, she called her doctor. After verifying the medication he was on and how long he'd been on it, the doctor gave her a few instructions. Hanging up, she returned her full attention to Thane.

"He says you need to ingest a lot of fluids."

A hazy grin took shape on his lips. "Ingest fluids? Is that a direct quote?"

Obviously, he had no idea how worried she was or he wouldn't make light of things. "Can I get you some water...or juice?"

"You don't need to do that," he drawled. "I will follow the doctor's orders, okay? And I'll lock the door once the room stops spinning." He aimed his unfocused gaze at her. "I'll even take a cold shower just to make you happy."

By this time, Naaki was certain he was hallucinating. Did he really think she could leave now? She couldn't have, even if she wanted to. She touched his face, a gesture she filled with all of her affections. "You should rest now. I'll make you something to eat."

His only response was a grunt, as his features relaxed to her caress. She watched him shut his eyes again and continued to stroke his face. Gradually, his breathing gained a steadier rhythm. Pressing a gentle kiss on his brow, she tried to ignore the tugging within her heart, the heart that now belonged to him. And that was the scariest thought.

With Thane asleep, Naaki's worrying began to subside, so she headed for the kitchen. She took a moment to look around and appreciate the room. It was an expansive space, at least one and a half times as big as her kitchen. There was a sense of warmth in the design and the harmonious olive and earth

tones, even without the much-needed personal touch, and she felt comfortable immediately.

She rummaged through the cabinets to
acquaint herself with where everything was.
A little more certain of her bearings, she decided to search the fridge. Earlier on when
she had put away Grace's fruits, she'd noted
it was newly stocked. Now she poked around
to see what she could find. There was a good
variety of veggies as well as some fish, so
she settled on soup. It was healthy, and even
if he had a bit of nausea—which she hoped
he didn't—soup would go down easily. Especially if she added a touch of spice.

She brought out the kitchenware she
needed from the cabinets and began her task,
pausing intermittently to check on him. Each
time it seemed more difficult to pull away
from his handsome face. Twenty minutes
later when she finished cooking, he was still
peacefully snoozing.

In spite of his quiescent state, he seemed
to exude a presence that was completely illogical. He was asleep, oblivious to the
world around him and...vulnerable. Yet he
commanded her attention and made her want
to do something about the heat pooling be-

tween her thighs. She shook away images of what that might entail and concentrated on the issue at hand. For a while, she considered waking him to eat. Eventually, she opted to let him rest.

To while away the time, she decided to retrieve her laptop from her car and set up in the dining room. Though it was a separate room, she could still see Thane, thanks to the open double-door separating the two areas. She took off her jacket and draped it over the back of the chair before sitting down. She was in for the long haul.

⁓⁓⁓

Thane woke up in waves of consciousness. First, came the general awareness of wakefulness. He was lying down. His ears picked up various sounds of the night before zeroing in on the faint music floating around him. He opened his eyes slowly, giving himself ample time to adjust to the dim light. The headache and dizziness had disappeared. Even though he had yet to take the evening dose of his medication, he felt more like himself. The doctor had been right on the mark when he'd predicted Thane would be feeling much better by this evening. He took in a deep breath.

A growl sounded from his midsection, drawing his attention to the vast empty pit in his stomach. A wave of queasiness made him groan. He needed to take in something quick before he collapsed again. The memory of his earlier fall brought on another more pleasurable memory. *Naaki.* His heart swelled with yearning, stopping his breath by the sheer force of it. She must be gone by now.

He shouldn't have asked her to stay. It wasn't as though he'd actually expected her to take him up on the offer, even though he was clearly in no condition to seduce her. She was too proper to disregard the implications of such an action, too smart to look impending disaster in the face and not try and save them both. She had made the right decision, of course. He knew that. But still all he could think about was the taste of her sensuous full lips, the warmth of her tongue, the gentle caress of her hands as they skimmed over his skin, her satisfied moan—even now the memory of it had his body pulsing with awakening need.

There was no getting around the issue. He wanted her. Remembering the intensity of her heated gaze when she said those three magical words—*kiss me, Thane*—he knew she wanted him as well. At least a part of her did. Where did they go from there? He couldn't pretend it didn't happen, neither could he act on it. Knowing she felt something for him, that she wanted him, complicated things. Because in five months, he would have to say goodbye.

As he sat up, he heard tapping sounds, like those made by a computer keyboard. Lifting his eyes, he saw her and started. The initial shock evaporated quickly, turning to joyous disbelief. He squeezed his eyes shut and opened them again. She was still there. He wasn't seeing things. It really *was* her. He frowned, wondering if he'd imagined her saying she couldn't stay.

She hadn't noticed him yet. Taking full advantage of that fact, he observed her as she worked on the laptop. Her jacket hung over the back of the chair. His gaze skimmed over the planes of her naked arms, wishing he could touch her right now. He took in the now-exposed body shaping top she wore, his eyes lingering on the alluring way the stretchy fabric gloved her breasts. Jealousy engulfed him. He wanted nothing more than to have his hand replace that fabric. He wanted to cup her breasts and feel her nipples harden against his palms, hug her while he was still bare-chested, know the texture of her silken skin more intimately. He yearned to discover how his name would sound on her lips while he made love to her.

Realizing his lips had parted just thinking about what he'd like to do to her, he clamped them, pushing the sexy images out of his mind. After all, none of it would happen. Because he couldn't go into a relationship knowing it had a limited shelf-life. Even if it was exactly what he wanted to do.

He knew the exact moment when she sensed he was awake, even before she turned. She stopped typing abruptly and frowned. Her chest rose gently as she took in a deep breath, capturing his interest for an instant. He was glad her eyes hadn't yet shifted to him or she'd have discovered just where his attention lay. When she turned, his focus was back up toward her face.

She released a breath, smiling at him in a way that had him thinking of homemade cookies, Christmas carols, and cuddling in front of the fireplace.

"You're awake," she noted, her soft voice solidifying the image of home and family swirling around in his mind.

"And you're still here."

He rose from his seat and made his way to where she sat. To her credit, though her expression mirrored concern, she made no move to assist. While he appreciated her concern and certainly enjoyed her company, he did not like to be babied. If she were his mother—which, thankfully, she wasn't—she'd have been fussing over him right now. But obviously she knew when to worry and when not to.

His progress was deliberately slow, since he still felt as if someone had reached inside him and taken out his internal organs, leaving him hollow. Had to be the hunger. When he sat down beside her, she turned to face him with one of those completely unguarded smiles she had that lit up the room.

"You didn't have to stay, you know," he said although he was damned glad she did. "I just needed to rest."

"I know."

"What are you typing?" he asked, changing the subject to avoid going down the emotional highway his mind was moving stealthily toward.

She shrugged, her attention still trained on him. "Just going through some reports I was working on today."

Though he recognized it was a good time to quiz her about work, since it would take his mind off how much he wanted her, work was the last thing he wanted to talk about.

"Are you hungry?" she asked, saving him from venturing into uncharted territory.

"Yes."

"Good, because I made soup."

"You did?" His mouth watered at the mention of food, while his stomach growled with eagerness. The fact that she'd cooked for him made him want her even more, but he tried to mask his emotions. "When I invited you to cook in my kitchen I'd hoped it would be under different circumstances." Being down with malaria was definitely not included in those circumstances. At the very least, he'd have liked to watch—er, help.

"You can always invite me back." A soft tint of color touched her cheeks.

His heart somersaulted, which should have worried him, since the last time he allowed a woman to get close, he'd only gotten pain and betrayal in return. But Naaki made him want, hope and believe, because she wasn't conniving and heartless. If she didn't want him, she wouldn't—unlike Arlene—lead him to believe she did and then walk off when a better deal came along. Hell, Brad Van Dusen was *not* a better deal. He had just a few more zeroes in his bank account. Pushing that unpleasant thought aside, he concentrated on Naaki. She could bet he'd extend the invitation again. In fact, he decided to do it now. "Done."

She smiled, hesitated a beat, and then she said, "I'll get the soup."

"Let me help."

She opened her mouth as if to protest then apparently changed her mind.

They returned to the table a few minutes later, each with a bowl of soup. The aroma rising from it was so appetizing, Thane couldn't wait to dig in. When he did take his first slurp, the taste exploded on his tongue making him shut his eyes to savor it. In the morning when he had attempted to eat, it all came back up after just a few bites. He waited for the nausea to hit, but nothing happened. The soup went down easily, its spiciness settling his stomach.

"This is really good," he commented.

"Thank you. I like cooking."

"My mom would love you." The words came out before he could stop himself. At least it didn't look like he'd freaked her out. "For her, everything is an excuse to cook or bake. Weddings, anniversaries, new neighbors."

"I cook when I'm nervous." She smiled. "It's therapeutic...creating something with my hands."

"Like art you can eat."

"Exactly." Her eyes widened. "That's it!"

He frowned. "What are you talking about?"

"Volta Foods' cookbook project we've been brainstorming on."

Volta Foods was one of the country's largest consumer food and body care manufacturers, holding its own against the local operations of global giants like Nestlé and Unilever. VF had contracted MIA to design a cookbook showcasing local recipes from all over West Africa along with tips for dressing the food for serving. It was a feeler project, which would determine whether the agency would be granted a retainer contract.

The past week, they'd been brainstorming on a tagline for the cookbook and come up with a few options they all liked but weren't crazy about.

"You're absolutely right," Thane said, his mind easily shifting gears to business mode. *Art you can eat.* He liked it.

He liked *her*. He enjoyed the way they could comfortably talk about both personal and business matters without feeling awkward. Okay, so they hadn't delved deeply into very personal stuff but it was because the relationship was new, not that the topic was uncomfortable.

As she jotted it down on her laptop, she commented on her expectations that VF would become a long-term client of MIA.

"Why do you like MIA so much?" Thane asked, unable to hold back his curiosity.

She paused. "They used to be number one, you know, and I wanted to be with the best." Finishing the note she was typing she went on, "But it's not just that. A lot of MIA's work put Ghana's advertising industry on the international map. Their mission is about developing groundbreaking communications that are still relevant to the market."

Thane couldn't help being lured by the passion in her voice. She had his full attention. "So it's a loyalty thing?"

"To an extent. MIA is still among the best in the industry despite its troubles. Many of the people there now were already with the agency in its glory days, so it's not a lack of talent as it is, perhaps, a lack of—"

"Direction?" Thane provided when she broke off.

"Exactly," she answered. "But now you're here. I honestly believe things are going to change quickly."

This wasn't the first time she'd alluded to her confidence in him and his plans for the agency. While he had no doubts about his own abilities, her belief in him made him want to ensure he didn't fail her. Right now, though, it was the discovery of her sense of loyalty that had him struggling to keep a tight rein on his emotions. She would be great not only as a co-worker but as a life partner. She wasn't the type who'd leave you behind when things got bad. She'd stay to slog it out with you.

Why did he have to meet her now, at a time and place where he couldn't do anything about it? *Dammit.*

# CHAPTER 13

When Naaki's eyes fluttered open the next morning, she was in a strange bed...a strange room. Her pillow was warm, comfortable and—she gasped—Thane's chest. Thane's *bare* chest. She shot a look down at herself. *Fully-clothed, thank God.*

How did she end up in his arms?

Last night after eating, Thane seemed to fare much better. He'd been adamant about giving her a quick tour of his new home after which they'd spent a few minutes discussing ideas for the cookbook project. At eight, he'd taken his medication as prescribed and they'd spent the rest of the evening talking.

She frowned, recalling how she'd insisted on making sure he went to bed. It had been after nine o'clock. They'd gone back and forth on that. Originally, he'd wanted to take the couch and leave her the bed, saying something about the spare bedroom being unfurnished. She didn't budge and, eventually, convinced him to take the bed. Being sick, he needed it more.

After winning that argument, she'd watched him fall asleep, fully planning on returning to the living room and sleeping on the couch.

Her eyes widened in shock as she remembered sitting on the other side of the bed, having succumbed to the urge to watch him sleep awhile. She must have nodded off, too—and in the middle of the night, she'd somehow rolled over to his side.

She tried to rise, but his arm, which she only now noticed was wrapped around her, held her firm. She went completely still for a second, catching her lower lip between her teeth. Don't wake up, she prayed. With any luck, she could get out without having to explain how they'd ended up in this position.

But, dear God, did it feel good to be in his arms. She could stay right there forever, listening to his heartbeat and slow breathing. Her fingers twitched and the texture of his soft chest hair made her want to run her hands over his whole torso. Every nerve-ending in her body became alert and wanting.

Reluctantly, she eased her face off his chest.

He groaned, pulling her back to his side. "Where d'you think you're going?"

*Uh-oh.* "I—err..."

"Good morning, beautiful." His voice was several octaves deeper than usual and it sent electricity straight down to her center.

"Morning." Now would be a good time to start explaining, she thought. "I, uh—"

Her voice caught when he started rubbing her arm with long tender strokes. She closed her eyes, her body trembling at his touch. A sigh sounded from her throat. She really could get used to this.

Thane's hand rose to her chin, lifting her face to meet his gaze. Her mind began to shut down when their eyes locked, and all the reasons why she should get up and run flew out of her head.

His hand came up further to tuck a lock of her hair behind her ears, letting his fingers graze her skin right at the base of her jaw.

"Is there someone in your life, Naaki?" His voice, thick with desire, wrapped around her like a gentle embrace. "A boyfriend?"

She shook her head, mesmerized. Her body was on fire, her heart threatening to break out of the confines of her chest. She was completely lost in the depths of his eyes, too weak to move.

"I don't have anyone either."

The air between them sizzled with tension and meaning. She saw it in his eyes, heard it in his voice. It was important for him to get that out of the way, to assure her they could have this moment. Nothing—no one—stood between them.

Emotion swelled in her heart, bubbling over as the fire in his eyes heated her blood. And she knew this was where she wanted to be. "Ok."

A breath rushed out of him as if he'd been holding it. He inched forward, closing the gap between them as he kissed her right eye shut, then the left. She stopped thinking—only felt—as his fingers ran lightly along the lines of her jaw, settling once more on her chin. She parted her lips, needing help with her breathing. He tilted her face further and kissed her cheek, her nose, then the corner of her lips, and she forgot to breathe.

Finally, he captured her lips. The contact melted her, body and soul. She whimpered and moaned, drinking him in. Her body trembled, filled with a voracious hunger she'd never experienced before—one that could only be sated by him. She plastered herself against him, sliding her hand around his waist as each fine swipe of his probing tongue made her even hungrier for more.

His hand curved around her shoulder, moving smoothly down the length of her arm. It settled on her hip, caressing her gently, pulling her further into him. Her thigh came into contact with his erection, and she sucked in a breath, as pressure mounted in her core. His warm caress moved up to her waist. The heat of his touch, radiating through the soft cotton fabric, warmed her to the marrow.

His hand skirted the outside curve of her breast, before his thumb ran lightly over her nipple, sending a sharp jolt of pleasure through her. She gasped.

"Naaki," he murmured.

Her attempt to say his name turned into a moan. She realized her mind was in no position to form words, so she concentrated on showing him what was in her heart—with her mouth and her hands.

A sound pierced through air...his cell phone ringing. He groaned his displeasure at the disturbance, pausing for only a second, then resumed kissing her with more ardor than before, determined to ignore the caller. The ringing didn't cease; instead but seemed to get louder.

Naaki was losing concentration fast. "Maybe you should get it," she said, hoping it would be a short call.

The ringing stopped abruptly.

Thane grinned. "Or not."

Just as their lips met again, the phone started ringing once more, causing him to pull back. Naaki stared into his eyes, disappointment cooling the hot yearning inside her. Clearly, the caller wasn't about to give up. And people like Thane didn't get unimportant calls.

"Excuse me," he said and reached for the phone. Taking a look at the number flashing, he shot her a regretful look. "I have to take this."

She nodded, already missing the warmth of his body. "Go ahead." She wanted to add,

I'll be waiting, but her brainpower had already kicked in, telling her the call had saved them from making an irrevocable mistake. Despite the heat still simmering right beneath the surface of her skin and the frustration torturing her mind, she slipped out of bed. Sliding her feet into her shoes, she ran her hands through her hair and straightened her skirt.

Thane's back was to her as he discussed something work-related. Naaki walked out of the room, stunned at how close she'd come to making love with Thane. Ignoring her feelings, she walked away from his steadily fading voice. She had to keep telling herself she was doing the right thing, even though each step she took away from him was harder than the one before.

Tears blinded her vision. She blinked them away, wondering if they were tears of disappointment or relief. A big part of her wanted to go back and pick up where they left off, damn the consequences, but she knew crossing that line could be dangerous. He was still her boss who inspired her confidence with his belief in her. She couldn't jeopardize that by allowing her emotions to dictate her actions. Not to mention how awkward it would be to work together after having sex.

Drawing strength from that knowledge, she picked up her handbag and laptop, then leaving a note on the dining room table, she walked out the front door.

の3の

"Thanks, buddy. I'll pick you up from the airport. Just shoot me an email when you finalize your flight details," Thane said, ending the call.

He didn't need to turn to know she wasn't there. He'd sensed her absence while on the phone but hadn't turned to check then, fearing he was right. Now he had no choice.

His heart tumbled, shoulders dropping ever so slightly when he looked around the empty room. He gave a regretful snort. Though he knew the outcome, he still searched the house, starting with the bathroom attached to his room and ending in the dining room.

She was definitely gone.

Pulling out a chair, he sat down. The joy that had fired the blood in his veins moments earlier had done a complete one-eighty, leaving him unsure of how he was going to endure the rest of the day. He'd spent the past week alone in this house and hadn't even noticed the silence. Yet in the few hours she'd been here, her presence had filled the rooms with life. And now the silence bothered him more than he cared to admit.

He covered his face in his palms and shut his eyes, welcoming the momentary darkness. It was time to take stock of this relationship—if he could call it that. Issues he hadn't considered before, because he'd been so bent on not falling for her, now plagued his mind—things like whether there was any rule preventing him from dating her. There was also Black & Black policy to consider. While no rule existed banning office romance, it was generally frowned upon—especially between people of unequal ranking.

It had never been an issue. And after Arlene's betrayal, he hadn't expected to fall in love again. He'd sworn not to put himself in a vulnerable position a second time, believing he'd never be able to trust a woman again. And with good reason. He'd put his complete trust in Arlene. He'd been on the verge of proposing to her. He'd gone through the trouble of secretly planning a romantic island getaway, where he'd envisioned basking in the sun together, sipping margaritas and making love. He'd even bought an expensive ring with an impressive rock—because Arlene didn't do subtle—planning to pop the question on the chartered flight to the island.

In retrospect, he'd been trying too hard. Perhaps deep down he'd always known she didn't love him. Maybe that was why he'd felt the need for an elaborate gesture to get her to say yes. His agony over Arlene's front-page wedding to Brad, when just four weeks before she'd been with him, had been needless.

To think he'd been so eager to sign his life away to that woman and never know he could have had better. With Naaki, there was no compulsion to impress. He was completely comfortable being himself around her. Now that he knew what it was like to wake up with her in his arms, to have her respond to him with so much passion—morning breath and all—he realized just what he'd been missing his whole life without even knowing it.

He pulled his hands halfway down his face, pressing his lips against his two forefingers. Who the hell was he kidding? Nothing had changed. He would still be leaving in five months' time. He cursed.

Opening his eyes, he noticed a small piece of paper. He frowned and picked it up. It was addressed to him. It had to be a note from Naaki. He opened it and read.

*I'm sorry.*

So was he. But probably for very different reasons. He wished there was something he could do to make himself forget how lousy he felt right now, fingering the note she'd left him.

❦

Naaki and Pat met for breakfast at their favorite café in town. It was Sunday—the day after Naaki woke up in Thane's bed—and the memories were still fresh in her mind.

"I'm impressed," Pat gushed as she listened to what Naaki had been up to while she'd been away. "Although I don't know if it's due to Thane Aleksander's ability to get you to stay at his place overnight or you daring to do so."

"It's nice to know how you've conveniently forgotten that I only stayed to take care of him," she joked, while staring dreamily over Pat's shoulder, remembering every detail of her sleepover at Thane's.

"Well, you did such a good job of it, he was well enough to make out with you in the morning," Pat teased.

"Nothing happened," Naaki said, although it felt good to be the one with a story for a change. Usually, she was at the listening end of her friend's escapades.

She, on the other hand, forever seemed to be in a stable relationship—using the term stable very loosely. Her whole life, there'd always been someone. First, her childhood sweetheart who had moved to another city with his parents when she was eleven; then nearly as soon as she started junior secondary school she became friends with a boy who remained her boyfriend for six years. All of these hadn't been serious relationships, more like special friendships that concluded naturally with the end of school or relocation of one. A few weeks into college, she'd met Gyamfi—her first actual relationship. She still wondered if she could really call him her first love.

"It seems to me like enough happened." Pat grinned, her eyes sparkling with excitement. "I can't believe this. I travel for a couple of weeks and you choose that time to have fun."

"Yes, well, his phone rang and—" She wanted to say *saved the day*, but knew Pat would just take that and turn it into a lecture, so instead, she said, "interrupted the fun."

"You could have waited." Typical Pat. She was sexually independent, went for what she wanted, when she wanted it. "Why did you leave when you so obviously like this guy?"

Naaki bit her lip, sighing heavily. "I got scared."

"Of what?"

"I don't know. I haven't got carried away like that before." She'd never met someone who could make her breathless just by looking at her—something Thane achieved on a daily basis with those shockingly gray eyes of his. "It's just—it's a huge step for me."

Pat placed a hand over Naaki's balled fist on the table, drawing her attention. "But you want to."

Naaki nodded. If only Pat knew how much she wanted to be with Thane, how hard it had been to drive away from his house yesterday. Talking about him now made her yearn to be back in his strong arms.

"I think I'm falling in love with him." Her pulse raced as she made this admission. "But what if it's a mistake? I want my first time to be with the right man, not someone who—" She broke off, looking down at her drink. "I don't want to have regrets."

"I see," Pat said knowingly. "You're scared he'll discard you after he's slept with you."

Heat crept up Naaki's neck, expanding steadily up her face. She felt terrible even considering the possibility. Thane didn't give her the impression of being someone who was out to use her. Why else would he go through the trouble of assuring her there was no one in his life? Then again, what did she know? She couldn't claim to be an expert where men were concerned. "That's not the only reason."

Pat waited for her to continue.

"Quite apart from, you know, doing it for the first time, it's going to be awkward going back to the office the next day and act as if nothing happened, especially if it turns out to be a mistake."

"It doesn't have to be that way. There are many people who've dated colleagues from work and ended up together," Pat argued. "What about couples who set up joint businesses? Sometimes having a personal relationship with someone actually enhances the experience of working together."

Naaki shook her head. "You're talking about partners. Thane is my boss."

"Technically, he isn't."

"What are you talking about?"

"You're on attachment. They don't pay you, so he may be the boss there, but he's not your boss."

"That's just calling it gray, Pat. Besides, I still have something to prove. I don't want people like Gyamfi thinking I only made it by sleeping with my superiors."

Pat threw her hands up in an exasperated manner. "Please tell me you're not seriously basing your decision on what Gyamfi will think. You're not responsible for what anyone chooses to believe."

Naaki went quiet for a while, tracing the edge of her glass as Pat's words hung between them. When she and Gyamfi broke up last year, she'd told herself it was important to take time off dating just to figure out who she was and what she wanted from life. Right now it meant focusing on her internship, and her certification and professional membership with the Chartered Institute of Marketing.

But then Thane had arrived and made her want both. He'd shown enough times how much he valued her input at work, throwing challenges her way that proved he trusted in her capabilities. When she wasn't contemplating how good it felt that he had so much faith in her, she couldn't stop appreciating his looks and the special way he made her feel when he touched her. She wrapped her arms around herself, rubbing away the goose bumps that claimed her skin from the memory of his sizzling kisses and his hands on her body.

"At the very least, have this experience for yourself," Pat said. "In a few short months he'll be gone and you'd have missed your chance."

The corners of Naaki's eyes twitched, and she suspected tears were imminent. Pat had a point. She didn't want to be left with regrets after Thane returned to the US, wishing she'd allowed her heart to love him without restraint. At the same time, the mere knowledge that he would leave in the foreseeable future already filled her with dread. She didn't know if she'd be able to watch him go with a piece of her heart.

"I still have my own expectations of me, and I'm the only one responsible for protecting myself from getting hurt."

"Look, Naaki, I'm not saying you should, by all means, date or sleep with Thane." Pat's tone was conciliatory as she gave Naaki's hand a gentle squeeze. "All I'm saying is, don't dismiss him for the wrong reasons."

# CHAPTER 14

I'm pleased to introduce my friend and colleague, Ty Webber," Thane announced to the team several days later. "Ty is an external auditor and financial consultant for Black & Black and will be working with the finance department here for two weeks. His assessment and report will help iron out some of the finer details of our partnership with Black & Black." He paused. *Our* partnership? Since when had he started counting himself as part of MIA and not Black & Black?

He scanned the faces staring back at him. It was difficult to tell whether anyone had taken notice. No doubt, there would be a sense of "us" versus "them" as was the case in most, if not all, negotiations. If perpetuated, that perception often delayed talks, with each party trying to ensure they didn't get screwed over. The solution was to establish trust early in the game and ensure all parties felt comfortable. It all came down to money—the reason why Ty was here.

It pleased Thane to note that the eyes looking back at him reflected optimism and anticipation—a contrast to the wariness he'd witnessed a few weeks ago. He hoped it meant they believed he had their interest at heart. When his gaze settled on Naaki, he faltered. Thankfully, it was only in his heartbeat—not his words. When she stared at him like that, with those brown eyes of hers radiating complete trust and admiration, it was all he could do to keep his distance. Tearing his eyes away, he brought his attention back to the meeting.

After his brief introduction, Ty stood up. "Thanks for the welcome. I'm glad to be here," he said. "The long and short of what Thane said is that Black & Black needs someone who can explain the books in a way that our American accountants can understand and vice versa."

Thane smiled. Ty often had an effective way of summarizing things. In this case, he was absolutely right. In addition to an MBA in Finance and a CPA, Ty had spent two years in Britain obtaining an ACCA—the equivalent of a CPA in the British-based education system—which put him in a unique position to understand the accounting practices here. While this was Ty's first official day at MIA, he'd been in town for a few days during which he'd gone through most of the background info Thane had put together. They'd also held private meetings with the accountants and a conference call with Steven Black.

Aside from being a consultant for Black & Black, Ty had been Thane's friend since college, where they'd been roommates for two years. Despite the warm welcome Thane had received so far, he was happy to have his friend here. It gave him a sense of control, even as he felt he was losing command of his emotions each time his gaze collided with Naaki's.

Since the day she woke up in his bed, he hadn't had a chance to talk to her alone. Though there was no uneasiness between them—at least not on his side—it killed him not knowing for sure that she was okay with what happened. *Or what hadn't happened.*

He hadn't felt this strongly about anyone before, hadn't wanted someone so much that it hurt. And yet he couldn't save himself by pretending she didn't exist. Just the sight of her filled him with more joy than he'd thought possible a few short weeks ago. Those precious moments he got to share a bit of his life with her made him feel so alive, it seemed better than not having her at all.

When the meeting ended a few minutes later, he walked out with Ty and Mr. Boateng, although at the back of his mind, he wondered how and when he would get Naaki alone again.

ⓔⓢⓔⓢ

Naaki shot a quick look around the creative studio before slipping into the archive room. She remembered the first day Thane brought her in here; how she'd been fascinated with all the old ad cutouts—and with him. Since then, she'd been in there a few times to search through old campaigns. That wasn't her focus now, though. She needed privacy to gather her thoughts.

A week had passed and yet nothing had changed. If anything, she was more drawn to

Thane than she thought possible. After his bout of malaria, he'd bounced back with incredible energy and the sparkle in his eyes was even more arresting. It had every nerve in her body stretched to its maximum.

She leaned against a wall unit and buried her face in her hands. The isolation offered little comfort as images of Thane refused to stay buried. Despite his impeccable business attires, all she could think of, all she could see, was the chiseled torso hidden beneath. She closed her eyes remembering the feel of his hard body under her palms. What would it be like to make love with him? The more she wondered, the more she desired to find out firsthand.

It was one of the reasons she'd done her best to avoid him this past week. It hadn't been as difficult as she'd expected, since he'd spent a greater part of the time working from home. But she knew her stroke of luck would end soon. There was no escaping the inevitable.

A noise at the door jolted her back to reality.

"My bad. I didn't realize someone was in here," Ty said, stopping abruptly. "I'll come back."

"No, no. Come in," Naaki said. As silence fell between them, she felt the need to say something. "I often slip in here to look at the old campaigns. Sometimes it helps in developing new ones."

"At the very least, you'll know what has been done before and avoid repetition." Ty cast a glance around. "Thane mentioned this room to me. He called it the hall of fame."

Naaki smiled, wondering how long the two men had known each other. After the meeting, she'd seen them chatting in the hallway over coffee. Their easy airs suggested they could be more than work colleagues. Now she watched him walk to one wall where the award-winning ads from the agency had been mounted.

Ty was African-American, about the same height as Thane, with the build of an American footballer. Though Naaki had never been attracted to bald men, she had to admit Ty's clean-shaven head and goatee suited him well. A gold stud in his left earlobe gave him a hip look usually not associated with accountants.

Unable to mask her curiosity, she asked, "How long have you known Thane?"

"A few years." He turned to face her, appearing unsurprised by her question. "We went to college together and have been friends since."

"So you have an ACCA," she stated, remembering the brief background Thane had given at the meeting. She was certain that ACCA wasn't recognized in the US. "How come?"

He shrugged. "I guess it was my way of getting in touch with my roots. I've always been interested in international business and finance. I toyed with the idea of spending a few years working in Africa. When I discovered the British system still prevailed in many African countries, I figured an ACCA would help." He chuckled. "Looks like I figured right."

Naaki nodded. "I'm working at getting a CIM certification. CIM is the marketing equivalent of an ACCA."

"Congratulations. Thane is one of the best people you could learn from anywhere in the world."

Her smile widened and her heartbeat soared at his words. "I'm confident that you and Thane being here is really good for MIA as well." She extended a hand. *"Akwaaba."*

"That's welcome, right?" Ty asked as he shook her hand.

Naaki nodded.

"How do you say thank you?"

"*Me daase.*"

Dipping his head slightly, he repeated, "*Me daase.*"

დოდო

Thane poured himself a cup of coffee though only one thing would calm him down—and she was somewhere downstairs. This was her week in the creative department. Although, today being Thursday, she had to stop by at some point with her progress report. He hadn't seen her since the meeting yesterday, and he couldn't wait for her to show up. Just as he set the coffee pot back down, Ty knocked and entered.

"What's making you so happy?" Thane asked, noting the pleased expression on his friend's face.

"I'm a Kwame."

Thane shook his head. Ty was big on being in touch with his roots. In the few days he'd been in Ghana, he already knew half as many local words as Thane. "Kwame" had to be his word of the day. "What's a *kwame*?"

"My Ghanaian name."

"And how do you figure that?"

"I was born on a Saturday," Ty replied. "Apparently, there's a name—male and female—for every day of the week, hence my Ghanaian name, Kwame."

Thane chuckled. "Coffee?"

"Nah, I'm good."

"Have a seat."

As Ty sat down and propped his laptop case against the chair, he frowned. "Man, you okay? Because you keep getting this far-away look in your eyes. Is there something going on?"

"What, you have a psych major I don't know about?"

"Very funny, bro. Take it from me. If you ain't getting any, the next best thing is to let out your feelings."

"Okay, Delilah." Thane quirked his eyebrows. "I hope you're not planning to 'hook' me up with anyone."

Ty looked deceptively shocked. "Now why would you accuse me of such a thing?"

"Labor Day weekend, Detroit. That ring a bell?"

"Come on, you can't fault a brother for trying. You were walking around angry with the whole damn world for what Arlene did to you. Man, you should be thanking me."

Thane snorted, remembering that weekend. Ty was right about him being angry. It had only been weeks since Arlene and her new husband's front page wedding. He hadn't yet gotten over the shock of losing her, when he discovered not only had she gone behind his back to steal his biggest client, she'd gone and married him too. It still pissed him off that he hadn't seen it coming.

He shook his head. "Such a waste." A waste of his time, effort, money and emotions.

"Tell me about it. I still had to pay Candy after you threw her out of your room."

"Serves you right," Thane replied unsympathetically.

"That's cold. Hugh Hefner woulda been grateful."

"Yeah well, that's the difference between Hugh and me." Thane sipped his coffee and scowled as he discovered it had turned lukewarm. "I don't need your help. Besides, I already met someone."

Ty sat up with interest. "You did? Who?"

261

Thane held up his hands to stop the train of conversation. "I'm not talking about this. Love is not on the agenda right now, so if you're not here to discuss work—"

"Pardon me for asking." Ty chuckled, recognizing the end of their moment of camaraderie. He produced his laptop. "If it's work you want, I've got plenty."

They went to work for forty minutes reviewing all the financial records and discussing them. Thane's suspicions that the agency was in a less than favorable state were confirmed. Ranking high among them were unpaid debts that seemed to have slipped through the cracks. Obviously, the previous management had exercised a lot of their veto power in dipping into the company's reserves. He could only be thankful that the accountant had kept meticulous records.

"Do you think we might have to let some people go?"

"Not enough to make a significant difference. What you need is to renegotiate payment plans for the debt or pay them off outright. For the size of the company, the debt is substantial, some overdue and gathering huge interests."

"I think MIA could use a deal where Black & Black recapitalizes the agency. That's the only way we can seriously negotiate more favorable repayment plans or even a payoff," Thane provided.

"Yeah, but that means a takeover." Ty dashed a glance at Thane. "I'm pretty sure MIA's owners would have something to say about that. Not to mention Black & Black."

"Yeah, you're right." An outright takeover was a big commitment. He wasn't sure Black & Black would go for it. Thane sat back, suspiring. "What we need is to get new clients into our portfolio. So far, there's only a few on the table."

Ty gave Thane a long, hard look. "You've been saying an awful lot of 'we' and 'our' in your discussions about MIA."

Thane leaned forward on his elbows, linking his fingers together. *Busted.* He rested the bridge of his nose on his knuckles.

I'm beginning to care about this place...and the people." He looked up. "It's getting personal."

"How come? You've always been all about the job. What's so special about Media Image Advertising?"

"Take anyone from here to the US, they'd earn twice as much as they get here, easy. And they are all salaried. No one earns over-time, but whenever there's work to be done, they're willing to stay late and come week-ends," he said.

"Good point, but you can't let this get personal."

"I know. It's just that I can't help think-ing MIA's already got the right bunch of people who'd be willing to put in the work required to make a real change." He sat back, resting his hands on the smooth surface of the desk. "But it's not just MIA. It's the Ghanaian culture, the spirit of community, the people."

One person in particular.

"I hate to be the devil's advocate here, but I'm an accountant and I got to say it. Take a step back, man. In the end, it's going to be about the bottom line."

"Don't I know it?"

"Good. Do me a favor and keep that in mind."

Thane laughed quietly as Ty gave him a good-natured pat on the shoulder. "I'm going to need another coffee." He stood.

Just as he reached the warm pot, there was a knock.

"Come in."

"Good afternoon."

The sound of Naaki's voice caused a radical jump in his heartbeat. He turned to look and froze. She was a vision, wearing a stunning white pant suit. He'd never seen her in pants before. It was one of those form-fitting, low-rise types with a jacket sitting neatly on the hip. The vibrant colors weren't missing, though. A flowery, chiffon shirt showed through the front V and bottom of the jacket. Her hair was tied back in usual fashion, leaving her brow-length bangs. Thane was completely floored.

Reaching for the coffee pot, his palm came into contact with the hot glass surface of the jar. He winced, snatching his hand away as the pain registered. He cursed, inspecting his palm. Luckily, it didn't look serious. Still, he went over to the fridge and got an icepack.

"I'm sorry. Are you all right?" Naaki asked, her eyes mirroring concern.

"Fine. It's nothing serious." Not compared to the havoc her appearance was having on him.

She gave him a small smile. "I—I just wanted to know when you'd like to do the progress meeting."

His gaze skimmed over her body. The fabric of her shirt was so light it had to be see-through. It took all of his willpower to gather his thoughts. "Uh, why don't you give me thirty minutes?" Hopefully, that was enough time to regain control of himself.

"Okay." She dropped her gaze, releasing him from her sensuous trap. "I'm sorry about the hand." With that, she left.

The sound of teasing laughter snapped Thane out of his semi-trance. He'd momentarily forgotten Ty was in the office.

"She's the one, isn't she?" Ty laughed again. "Man, you're whipped."

Thane ignored the gibe as he poured himself a fresh cup of coffee.

"At least she likes you, too. I've never seen two people practically strip each other naked with their eyes," Ty mocked. "No need to explain why things are getting personal."

Still remaining quiet, Thane sipped his beverage. There was no sense in denying the accusation or encouraging them.

"I officially apologize for Candy." Ty chuckled, but didn't get a response from Thane. "So why the long face?"

Thane sighed. "There's no point in starting anything with her when in little less than five months I'll be back home."

"Man, are you listening to yourself? That was the plan before you met her. Plans are like forecasts; they're meant only as a guide." Ty punched the table with his forefinger as he spoke. "There's no law that says she can't go with you."

Thane shook his head. "You're assuming she wants to come with me."

"I'm assuming she's also whipped." Ty stood, packing his laptop. "Have you asked her?"

Thane found himself seriously considering the option. Would she be willing to start over? New country? New job? New friends? It seemed too much to ask. There was no guarantee she felt the same way about him. She *did* leave his bed the other day.

"There's always long distance," Ty continued.

"Being with her and yet not *being* with her? Not gonna work."

Ty shrugged as he turned towards the door. "Do yourself a favor, my friend. Ask yourself if she's worth a change in your big plan."

∽∾∽∾

Thirty minutes later, Naaki was going over her report with Thane, reiterating some of the details while he scrolled through the document. By now, she was used to him taking charge of the mouse, which meant she had to scoot closer to read her own report. On a few occasions, she'd wondered whether the nearness was his intended objective or if he had a version of the "remote control syndrome."

An image of fighting him for the remote popped into her mind, causing her to stifle a giggle. Of course, she wouldn't squabble with him or resort to trickery, for that matter. She'd just get a spare—something no one seemed to think of. There were bound to be more fun activities they could do together.

She couldn't keep the smile from her voice, however.

Thane looked at her curiously. "What's funny?"

"Nothing."

He nodded, but his skeptical look indicated he didn't buy her response.

"I'm just happy." It was a hundred percent true, though she prayed he wouldn't ask her why. She wasn't quite ready to confess how much being here with him filled her heart with gladness.

His eyes softened as his lips curved up. "I'm happy too."

Warmth spread from her polar regions and pooled in a heat wave of arousal in her middle. Could it be that she made him happy too? She wanted to ask, but stopped herself, choosing to follow his example and return her attention to the report.

When they finished a while later, Thane copied the document onto his machine, ejected her thumb drive and handed it to her.

"You know, it's considered ill-mannered to hand out anything with your left hand?" She kept her tone light to let him know she was merely making conversation.

"Really?" He seemed fascinated by the thought. "Even if my right hand is occupied or my left is closer to the person I am giving it to?"

She nodded. "In either case, you'd have to apologize for using your left."

"Why?" Understandably, he appeared blown away by the idea.

A blush heated her face as she answered. "Because it's the one used when you go to the loo."

He burst out laughing, which made her feel completely silly. However, his unrestrained laughter was infectious, and soon had her breaking into a few giggles.

"Please accept my sincere apologies for using my left hand," he said.

Naaki chuckled.

Speaking of his left hand, that was the same one he burned.

"Can I see your hand?" She'd wanted to ask before but thought it might be somewhat inappropriate, maybe unprofessional. After mentioning "loo," though, revealing her concern didn't seem out of place.

He fanned out his fingers, showing her his palm. "It's fine." His voice was a gentle caress, turning the moment into something intimate.

She placed her hand in his, using her fingertips to rub gently. "No pain?"

"None." His voice had turned gruff, making her all too aware of their closeness.

She raised her eyes and noticed him watching. Her body hummed with already awakened need. He closed his hand around hers, caressing the back of it with the pad of his thumb. Her body responded with subtle shivers that had her melting inside. Their hands moved in unison, their fingers intertwining, seemingly propelled by their own desires.

His eyes didn't leave hers as he continued to rub her hand. He slipped his thumb into her palm and her throat went dry. Luckily, she still had the presence of mind to stop herself from closing her eyes and letting the sensation overtake her. Although, now that her fingers were acting of their own accord, it was as if their hands were determined to demonstrate the kind of harmony they should be working on.

This is crazy, she thought. They were in the office; any one could walk in. But, ooh, this did feel strangely, wonderfully, innocently good. She sucked in a breath, capturing her lip in her teeth. Her eyes began to shut as her thoughts fizzled out of her mind.

He applied pressure to his thumb so his nail grazed her soft palm, shooting darts of shivers through her. She gasped. Her eyes flew open. Her mind began to function again. What was she doing? His touch made her forget herself, made her want to throw caution to the wind. But she couldn't afford that—not when she had a career to pursue. With his career already established, he had nothing to lose.

"Thane." She blinked and disengaged her hand, shaking herself mentally to escape the hypnotic effect of his stare. She stood, but any plans of leaving ceased when his hand closed around her arm. Her eyes shot up to meet his gaze.

"What are you afraid of, Naaki? Why do you keep running from me?"

"Because—" Her voice caught as she tried to temper her racing heart. "This can't happen." *Please understand.*

Silence hung between them waiting to be broken by his response.

He let out a heavy breath. "I know." His voice was no louder than a whisper.

"I have to focus on building my career."

"Me, too." Despite his words, he didn't release her.

"I—I can't be distracted."

"Me neither," his gaze swept over her frame before returning to her eyes, "but when you dress you like this, I can't help being distracted."

She looked down at the suit Pat had brought her from Cape Coast. Trouser suits, especially white ones, weren't her preferred choice of clothing. Disappointment sliced through her. Was everything that had just happened due to her outfit? What had she expected? She should have known better than to entertain any feelings for him.

"It doesn't really matter what you're wearing," Thane confessed. "You'd look good to me in anything."

Of all the things she could have imagined, she wouldn't have guessed this. Words escaped her. Whatever she'd been thinking earlier, he'd just shot down with one statement.

"I care about you, Naaki." The sincerity in his unwavering gaze told her he was dead serious. "I didn't expect to care about any woman again. The plan was to come to Ghana, complete my negotiations and go back home. But I met you and things don't seem so simple anymore."

She opened her mouth but no sound came out.

"Please understand that my actions have never been meant to hinder your progress or distract you." He released her. "You're right. This shouldn't happen."

With that, he walked out leaving her alone in his office. Her mind buzzed as if every tiny cell in her brain was vibrating with new life. Although she still couldn't garner enough strength to move her limbs. Thane cared about her, yet he agreed that whatever was happening between them had no future. She should have been happy.

But all she wanted to do was cry.

# CHAPTER 15

There was only one word to describe Thane's weekend—lousy. He'd spent the entire time grappling with mixed emotions, missing someone who was never his to begin with. His chest nursed a dull ache as though his heart was coming apart. He'd lost count of the number of times he'd fought the urge to go back and tell her he'd changed his mind.

Even as he eased his car into the parking lot on Monday morning, he had to resist following Ty's advice each time it popped into his mind with its sweet temptation. He paused briefly at the reception to ask Aku about her weekend—one of the habits he'd picked up since arriving. He'd discovered that greeting was a big thing here. It was

Empi Baryeh

even considered rude to pass someone on the street without some form of salutation.

Leaving a beaming Aku to her duties, he dropped his briefcase in his office, passed by Mr. Boateng's to exchange a few pleasantries and headed to the creative studio. Usually, he'd spend a few minutes in his office checking mail, knowing most of the staff would drop by to say hello. But today he couldn't wait. He was too anxious to find Naaki, although he didn't know what he'd say, if anything. He hadn't decided what to do about their mutual agreement to be apart. He knew, though, *something* had to be done about that persistent emptiness he felt inside. Something like seeing her—even for a few minutes. He'd convinced himself if he had enough of staring at her, it would be sufficient to keep him going after he returned to the US. Of course, he knew a lie when he heard it.

But he wasn't going to dwell on that just yet.

He punched the four-digit code and heard the studio door open with a click.

He stepped in. At the sight of her, his breath snagged. She was seated next to Jeremy, the creative director, as he explained something to her. Thane took in the curves of her profile. Something shifted in him. How could he ever hope to function on images stored in his mind when reality never ceased to trump memory?

"Good morning, Thane," one of the designers said, alerting the others to his presence.

Since he was already looking at Naaki, her gaze easily captured his. "Hi," he answered.

Greetings were chorused across the room, but he only heard hers—even though her lips didn't move. Her eyes sparkled as warmth seeped into their depth. She was happy to see him. A gush of emotion coursed through him in response.

A movement in the corner of his eye brought his attention to Jeremy who had just placed his hand on Naaki's shoulder. A visceral surge of possessiveness gripped Thane. His heart tightened, and he had to resist the urge to rip the guy's arm off. He noticed Naaki stiffen. She lifted her shoulder slightly. Perhaps a polite gesture to tell the guy to take his paws off her? Obviously the sleazebag didn't speak polite.

He made his way to them. "What's up?" Though he tried to maintain a light air, there was still an edge to his voice.

Jeremy's hand immediately slipped off Naaki's shoulder as he explained what they were reviewing. Something about three design proposals for the "art you can eat" cookbook. Thane wasn't paying attention. Naaki was looking at him, her eyes filled with relief and...gratitude? He winked and her cheeks flamed with color as her eyes widened. A smile tugged at the corners of his lips. He'd never tire of seeing her blush.

He leaned in to take a closer look at the computer screen, pretending he wasn't more aware of the woman next to him than the screen or that he wouldn't rather whisk her off to somewhere private and forget all talk about work.

Two hours later, Thane was agitated, unable to get her out of his mind. Not that he really wanted to, but after getting off the phone with Steven Black, he felt a little disoriented. Though a part of him remained abuzz from seeing Naaki earlier, another part was getting increasingly frustrated with the Black brothers. His conversation with Steve left him with a suspicion that they were rethinking the relationship with MIA. He couldn't let that happen, not just because he actually believed it was a viable venture, but because it meant cutting his trip short. *That* prospect had him on edge as he paced the breadth of his office.

He didn't want to think that the time to say goodbye to Naaki could be much closer than he thought. He didn't *want* to say goodbye. Yet he'd agreed with her assertion that nothing good could come of them giving in to their feelings.

She was strong—obviously. He wasn't.

Another reason why he wanted to see as much of her as he could before they were inevitably separated, why he continued to burn holes in the carpet, trying to control the emotional rollercoaster roiling within.

He gave up trying. He was going in search of her again—to tell her he'd changed his mind. He wanted her. They'd just have to figure out how to make it work. He was a world-class negotiator, dammit. He didn't run from challenges.

Buoyed by that thought, he headed out of the office.

⸾ↄⸯↄ

Naaki wasn't about to admit it, but she was hiding out. Though she preferred to think of it as recuperating; her heart needed a timeout after all the pounding it had done that morning. So instead of staying in the office, she'd retreated to the boardroom to review some research reports.

Assimilating the information wasn't difficult although the task of suppressing thoughts of Thane had reached a new level of impossibility. Nothing she tried seemed to work. Not while she kept picturing how gorgeous he looked. When he winked, it had caused a stirring in her chest. She'd felt as though he'd read her thoughts, sensed her discomfort and come to her rescue. Funny how the idea didn't set off any "damsel in distress syndrome" alarms. She could have resolved the situation on her own, yet somehow having him step in had given her a sense of belonging, as if for the first time she was part of a team—a two-person team. She liked that. She liked *him*.

Now, it was past ten o'clock and she still hadn't managed to wipe the goofy grin off her face. Neither had she been able to stop the overwhelming desire to truly be one with Thane. She pondered his question about her reasons for running from him. She'd thought of nothing else the past few days, questioning every reservation she harbored—her concerns of becoming intimate with him and realizing it was a mistake, fears of her feelings developing to the point where she'd be willing to give up anything to be with him— including her career, which was the one thing she could count on. Then there was the need to prove she made the grade based on her professional capabilities and not any personal relations with the boss. But Thane hadn't done her any favors. Despite what they'd shared outside of work, he gave equal regard to each person's contribution. The more important thing, though, was that he *did* believe in her.

Not only him; everyone else valued her input. Case in point, the strategic planner was the one who'd requested her help with reviewing the research data currently in front of her.

It all made her question herself. Did she really have to sacrifice love and family for career? Had Gyamfi's constant badgering about career being only for the tough at heart affected her more than she imagined? She thought she'd escaped that relationship—*that trap*—before any damage could be done. Now as she reflected on it, she couldn't help wondering if somewhere in her subconscious she lacked faith in herself. She chuckled. She'd have thought someone with the middle name Faith would be above having that particular problem.

She'd just finished jotting some points in her notebook when she had a sensation of being watched. She raised her head and found Thane leaning against the door jamb, his arms folded. He looked larger than life—and completely irresistible.

"There you are." His voice was like a gentle breeze on a hot day, and the sparkle in his eyes mirrored the joy brimming in her heart. "What are you doing?"

Heat curled in her lower abdomen as their gazes met. She cleared her throat to make sure her voice was still there. "I'm looking through some consumer Usage and Attitude reports."

"The U&As? I wanted to see them. Mind if I join you?"

*Mind?* She shook her head. "Not at all." She waved her hand over one small pile of papers. "I'm done with these, so you're welcome to them."

He sat next to her.

A silent shiver spread through her. He was so close, she didn't need to lean in to catch a whiff of his smell, enhanced by a subtle masculine fragrance. She did, any-way—slightly—when she handed over the pile she'd indicated. The heady warmth of his nearness was delightful. She made no at-tempt to squash the sensation, knowing any such effort would be futile.

He received the sheets, but set them aside. Instead, his eyes remained focused on her. "Have you ever considered pursuing your career elsewhere? Outside Ghana?"

Her response was immediate. "No." She didn't need to think about it. But when dis-appointment flashed in Thane's eyes, she had a feeling she'd given the wrong answer.

"Why not?" Thane pressed. "Don't you think there's a lot out there that you can learn?"

"I do. In fact, I've attended several con-ferences outside Ghana for exactly that pur-pose, but I've never imagined my life any-where else."

He sat back. This time the disappointment lingered as a frown touched his brows.

"I dream of getting into tourism." When his frown further deepened in incomprehension, she explained, "Tourism marketing. When people want to visit Africa, they think of the Serengeti and safaris. Ghana doesn't have the kind of wildlife you find in East and Southern Africa, but we do have a lot of other very unique attractions that many people, even here, don't know about."

He nodded attentively, urging her to continue.

"Thirty years ago, who'd have thought of a desert country as a tourist destination? But look at Dubai today. Egypt is promoting itself too. My ultimate hope is to put my country on the world tourism map."

She'd never revealed her dream to anyone aside from her best friend, but she found herself wanting to share it with Thane. "I want people to see what I see, feel what I feel when I think of Ghana, and to celebrate the uniqueness of our culture with us."

Her heartbeat surged with excitement. She paused, wondering whether she was getting carried away. Surely Thane wasn't interested in her lofty dreams. Yet he nodded as if he understood. She could have sworn his look held admiration.

"That's impressive," he said. "Is it why you feel a relationship will distract you?"

His question made her falter. When he looked at her the way he did right now, like he was in awe of her, it made it easy to believe he'd be willing to support her ambition. So instead of an outright "yes," she said, "It *is* an ambitious dream."

"But not impossible."

Naaki swallowed. She'd half expected him to convince her to think smaller. Because her dream meant first convincing state and private organizations to set aside funds to develop the tourism industry, to provide facilities that would ensure the sites were safe and accessible to tourists. All of that needed to happen before promoting the country abroad. But she felt strongly enough about it that she was willing to put in the work.

"You don't think I'm setting myself up for disappointment?"

He shook his head. "That's exactly where you're missing the point, sweetheart. When people have the passion to do something, there aren't many things that can get in their way. Besides, you don't have to do this alone." He smiled. "Part of being a good

285

marketer is to be able to convince people to join your cause."

"You make it sound so simple."

He shrugged, and Naaki couldn't help feeling something in his disposition had changed. It appeared as though, for the first time, he wasn't holding back. "Are you passionate about this dream?"

"I am."

"Then it's simple."

There it was again, that goofy smile. It felt goofy; she hoped it didn't *look* it. Although she didn't care. She was simply happy to know for sure that he had faith in her abilities. He was the smartest, most supportive man she'd ever met. And he didn't think her dream was far-fetched. All this, coupled with the potent chemistry between them, made it impossible to resist. Her heart thickened with emotion, and she realized she'd already fallen in love with him.

"What about you?" she asked. "Do you have a lofty dream?"

"I don't know about it being lofty, but I do want to make a name for myself. Someday people will want affiliation with an agency that has my name on it." He looked right into her eyes, his expression earnest.

"Maybe I'll even write a few books on Advertising."

"If anyone can do it, you can."

The corners of his eyes crinkled slightly, as his lips curved up briefly, then his expression changed to something intense.

"Naaki." Whatever was coming had to be serious. "I'd like to take you out on a date."

*On a what?* Stunned, Naaki could only stare back as her heartbeat escalated. "A—a date?" She couldn't have heard right.

"I know you're focused on building your career, and I fully support it, especially now that you've told me more." His look turned even more earnest. "Here's the thing. This whole weekend I thought of nothing except you, and I realized I don't want to ignore my feelings."

Her mental faculties were back to working in full force, but her head was crowded with questions, and her mind hadn't managed to string together two words. She couldn't believe Thane was really asking her on a date. *A date.* And he was telling her the same things she'd thought about over the past few days.

"I couldn't help asking myself if we're bailing out of a good thing. Isn't it possible to have both a personal and a professional relationship?" He took her hand. "We both have dreams we want to pursue, and if you really think I'll hinder your progress, then say no, but I know I want you, Naaki. This doesn't have to be a distraction."

*No, it doesn't.* In fact, fighting the attraction between them left her more off-balance. She'd already given her heart to him. It should have scared her, because the possibility of getting hurt when Thane finally left had become a reality. But it only made her want to take advantage of what little time she had. She loved him, and even though he hadn't said he loved her too, she was certain he wouldn't sidetrack her—unless it was in reference to the effect of his kisses.

"I couldn't stop thinking about you either." At her words, Thane's look grew more tender, melting her insides. "So yes. I'd like to go on a date with you, Thane."

"How does eight o'clock, Saturday sound?"

"What about Friday? It's a holiday." Now that they had a date, she couldn't wait. Saturday was too far. "Seven?"

"Friday, seven it is. Dress up." He gave her hand a gentle squeeze. "I'll drive."

❧❧❧

*Almost time.* After all the restlessness, the figurative nail-biting, Friday evening was here. Naaki's heart hammered an erratic beat. She tried not to count down, even though time couldn't go any slower. She diverted her attention to the soft music streaming from her home theatre system—a CD Pat brought, insisting the hypnotic instrumentals had a calming effect. Since it didn't seem to be doing anything for her wired nerves, Naaki decided it was probably some gimmick they taught at beauty school to justify their professional rates.

She was glad to have her friend around, though. Not just because Pat was a beauty consultant and had promised to make Naaki look "perfect" for her date. Having someone around made the wait more bearable. Although the nail treatment, the face and foot massages, and now makeup made Naaki feel like she was trying too hard. It certainly did nothing to calm her racing pulse.

"You're fidgeting again." Pat held an eyeliner brush a couple of inches from Naaki's face. "Be still. These are very dangerous instruments I'm using."

Naaki snorted, desperately grasping at the lighthearted remark. Anything to keep her mind off the clock. "Ooh, makeup tools. Scary."

"Laugh all you want, woman. But I wouldn't be so eager to mock anyone holding a sharp instrument next to my eye." She flashed a quick grin before commanding, "Eyes closed."

Naaki gave an exasperated sigh before doing as she was told. "I'm nervous. I've never spent two hours getting ready for anything." *Or anyone.* An all-too-familiar warmth suffused her body. She'd never yearned for someone the way she craved Thane right now. She wanted simply to be in his presence, to gaze into the vast intensity of his eyes, feel his touch...his kiss. "I'm sure it wouldn't even make a difference to him. He'll probably not notice."

"Trust me, he will." The gentle strokes of a contour brush touched Naaki's face as Pat applied a light coat of loose powder.

"Maybe that's what I'm afraid of." Though she'd meant her reply as a joke, her voice trembled. She didn't doubt her friend's skill for one minute. Pat was good at what she did. And she took pride in her job. She'd done makeup for countless brides, including several prominent celebrities, not to speak of the pictures of other clients lining one wall of the little work area in her flat. So there was no need to be anxious about the mirror being behind her rather than in front of her. Pat didn't want her "monitoring" the process.

"Don't worry, I'm a professional," Pat assured, the smile in her voice evident. "I promised to make you look perfect for Thane and that's what I'm doing."

For whatever reason, despite her impressive portfolio, Pat had been dying for an opportunity to do Naaki's makeup. Special occasions were her strong suit, and since they both agreed this occasion was special, Pat couldn't be talked out of the idea.

Naaki inhaled deeply, resigned to her fate. "I trust you."

Pat laughed. "You sound *so* convincing. I'm touched."

Naaki smiled. If her eyes weren't shut, she'd have rolled them. She was about to say something when Pat spoke again.

"All done."

Naaki opened her eyes. Pat stood, arms folded, eyes twinkling, beaming like a child in front of a birthday cake. The pleased expression gave Naaki some comfort. Her best friend wouldn't allow her to go out looking like a mannequin.

"Feel free to take the credit for how gorgeous you look."

"You think I look gorgeous?"

"Stop fretting and turn around. See for yourself." Without waiting for a reaction, Pat grabbed the chair and swiveled it around bringing Naaki face-to-face with her image in the large dressing mirror.

She stared at herself, blinked. Her lips parted as she sucked in a breath. That couldn't be her. Could it? Once she got over the purple eyeliner, she began to appreciate its effect in bringing out the browns of her eyes. With a gentle blush kissing her cheekbones and a soft natural look for her lips, the effect was stunning. She had to be wearing more makeup than she'd ever done before, yet it didn't feel or look that way. Her bangs, together with the rest of her hair, had been swept up into a stylish do, opening up her face and accentuating her features.

"My eyes..." She'd always thought them quite ordinary, yet right now she couldn't help feeling like she was really seeing them for the first time.

"I told you I knew what I was doing." Pat lowered herself onto a foldable chair next to Naaki.

This time Naaki did roll her eyes. "I'm sorry if I sounded like I doubted your abilities."

Pat chuckled. "You did look worried when I walked in with my professional kit, but you didn't expect me to show up with only my quick-fix pouch, did you? Now, let's get you dressed. We don't want you running around in a bathrobe when Thane arrives."

*Well...* "No, we don't," she agreed, at the same time imagining herself greeting Thane clad just that way.

But since she had a date to attend, she shoved the enticing notion out of her mind and went to her wardrobe for her evening gown; a two-piece ensemble, consisting of a long multi-layered chiffon skirt and corset-style top with capped sleeves. The top was made from a special *kente* fabric, created with purple and gold threading that glittered when the light caught it.

Donning that, she then slipped her feet into a pair of strappy gold sandals. With the length of her skirt, only the amber-colored polish on her toenails could be seen. Her necklace, a half-moon pendant cradling an amethyst, her birthstone, hung from a thin gold chain. She added matching earrings. "What do you think?"

Pat's eyes filled with warmth. "Gorgeous." She made a weepy face and sniffed, wiping away imaginary tears. "My little girl is all grown up."

"Not too much?" Naaki stood in front of the mirror for a final inspection. "He did say to dress up."

"And when a man tells you to dress up, there's no such thing as too much."

Naaki shook her head and chuckled, but before she could respond a light from outside flashed across her window, then they heard the sound of a car's engine.

"He's here." She'd thought her previous case of nerves was bad, but now her heart went wild, the wave of excitement almost making her lightheaded.

They walked into the living area together. A gentle tap on the front door came moments later.

"Just a minute," Naaki called out, then turning to Pat, she said, "Hide."

"What? No," Pat protested although she retreated to the kitchen, where she could spy without detection.

Naaki swung the door open and had to take a step back at the sight of the man standing in front of her. Any worries about being over-dressed oozed out immediately. His clean-shaven look complimented the formal attire he wore—tuxedo with a dress shirt and bow tie. He exuded power and sensuality all in one sexy package.

He seemed to fill the space with his broad shoulders and tall frame. Even with the boost of her two-inch heels and a one-step floor elevation, she had to look up to meet his gaze. Heat flared within, turning her insides to mush. He looked...

"Wow." That was the word in her mind, but it was Thane's voice which spoke as he did his own bit of staring. "You look amazing."

*Amazing.* The word she was looking for. "You too."

He smiled, extending his arm, which was hidden behind him. "These are for you."

Naaki's eyes widened. In his hand was a bouquet of a dozen perfect red roses. Without warning, a lump formed in her throat.

She'd never thought of herself as a flowers person. Apparently, she was.

"Thank you. These are beautiful," she said, receiving them.

"They don't compare to you."

By now, tingles and thrills were an expected reaction to Thane. But his comment filled her with a sudden intense heat, she wondered how many more of such remarks she could take before she eventually combusted.

"I'll put them in water." She held the door open for him to enter.

While Thane waited in the living room, Naaki went to the kitchen where Pat took charge of the bouquet and shooed her away.

# CHAPTER 16

After fifteen minutes in the car, Naaki gave up trying to guess where he was taking her. They were going in the opposite direction of most of the five-star restaurants in the city. She wracked her brains for eating places she may have missed, ones that matched their dress code, but came up short. It looked like they were headed out of town.

"Where are we going?" she finally asked.

"It's a surprise." Thane glanced at her and all thought flew out of her mind. "You'll like it."

Naaki decided it didn't matter where they were going as long as they were together. Her heart rate stepped up a notch. She couldn't wait for the surprise.

After another forty-five minutes of driving and general conversation, they turned off the main road. Up ahead was an open gate with a security post beyond which street lights made it easy to see the grand palms flanking each side of the drive. *No way*. Only one place was famed for having the palm tree drive. The mountainous road they'd used should have alerted her, but she hadn't been paying attention. Once she'd decided to stop guessing where they were headed, the conversation had taken over.

The sign came into view, eliminating the need for speculation—*Aburi Botanic Gardens*. She didn't speak, still unable to believe he'd brought her to one of the most famous tourist destinations in the country. It dated back to mid-nineteenth century, making it one of the oldest national landmarks. She couldn't have picked a better place herself.

"Good surprise?"

"Perfect surprise," she replied, though she still wondered if they weren't a tad—maybe a lot—over-dressed.

"There's more." They'd just parked. When she made a move to open the door, he stopped her. "Let me get it."

She sat in the car watching as he came around to her side and opened the door. She got out, taking the arm he offered. Stepping onto the paved walkway, they didn't go towards the main restaurant building, but rather away from it. Garden lamps lit the way, though they made the exotic vegetation beyond appear as silhouettes in the dark.

Curiosity mounted, but she refrained from asking. She trusted his choices. He'd already proven he knew how to impress her. They rounded a corner and she gasped, believing only because she was seeing it—*it* being a resplendent gazebo in the middle the garden ahead. She paused, taking in the sight. Lit by tiny bulbs nestled in bougainvillea arranged around its pillars and rails, the gazebo stood out like a castle on top of a hill. Around it were insect repellant lamps. A formal dinner setting lay within—a table for two. From somewhere, soft music started playing. She felt like she'd just stepped into a fairytale.

"Thane, this is gorgeous."

He turned towards her, meeting her gaze. "I'm glad you like it."

Naaki allowed herself to be led into the gazebo. She sat on the chair Thane pulled out for her and watched him take the opposite seat. Seemingly out of nowhere, two waiters appeared to take their orders. The meal started with a crisp garden salad, followed by a local recipe of eggplant soup, fillets of charcoal-grilled Tilapia with ground hot pepper on the side and steamed vegetables. Dessert was a tropical fruit bowl.

After the table was cleared, Naaki's bubbliness diminished though she tried not to show it. Dessert meant the end of the meal; the end of the date. She didn't want the evening to end, didn't want to go back to Accra tonight.

Thane reached across the table and took her hand as silence settled over them. He met her gaze and smiled. It was a slight one, but the tenderness in his eyes spoke to her very heart. Despite the cool mountain temperatures, her body began to heat up from the spot where his thumb rubbed the back of her hand.

"I didn't know they had gazebos here," she commented, hoping the conversation would make him forget about heading back if only for a few minutes. "It must be a new feature."

"It's a temporary feature. I had it made for today." He brought her hand to his lips and pressed a kiss into her palm.

Recovering from the jolt of electricity that simple gesture elicited, Naaki had to make an effort to raise her voice above a whisper. "You didn't have to go through all that trouble for me," she said, although it made her feel special and giddy inside. "Any restaurant in Accra would have been enough."

"I know, but none of them would have put that radiant smile on your face." He'd moved from rubbing the back of her hand to tracing circles along her arm. "In case you haven't noticed, I like putting smiles on your face."

Her smile brightened. "It's wonderful. I've had a great time."

"Me, too." The corners of his lips lifted slightly. "Would you like to dance?"

Apparently she wasn't alone in her desire to extend the evening. "I'd love to."

Still holding hands, they rose and stepped away from the table. Thane spun her around once before pulling her to himself. His right hand settled on her back, high enough for the tips of his fingers to brush her skin. All evening Naaki had wanted to be in his arms and now that she was, the hunger erupted. Each part of her that touched him acted as a conductor, transmitting heat from his body into hers.

His fiery gaze told her the desire wasn't one-sided. He pulled her closer, letting his hand slide to the small of her back. His hardness pressed against her abdomen, and her body responded with an ache in the sensitive areas between her thighs.

"You feel so right in my arms." His voice, low and husky, fanned the flames of desire burning within her. His breath against her face made her tremble.

She snuggled closer, telling herself to enjoy this moment and not worry about how close to completion the night was. "I like being in your arms, Thane."

"Then why is there sadness in your eyes?"

Was she so easy to read? What else could he detect in her eyes? "I don't want the evening to end."

"It doesn't have to."

She frowned, puzzled. "Don't we have to be returning soon?"

"Not tonight."

A glimmer of hope flickered. "Are you saying—"

He didn't allow her to complete her question. "We're staying. I reserved two chalets in case you wanted to stay."

*Two?* Naaki's stomach sank. *Of course.* What had she expected? Thane was nothing if not a gentleman. He wouldn't book them in one room without asking.

"Oh." She hated the disappointment she heard in her voice.

His next statement took care of her follow-up question. "Your friend Patricia packed a weekend bag for you. It should already be in your room."

Pat? "How did you—" She broke off, remembering Pat and Thane had indeed met on Tuesday. Pat had claimed to have a job in the neighborhood, but Naaki suspected her friend had another motive. On Monday, when Naaki had told her about the date, Pat had commented about the need to scope out Thane—*make sure his intentions are honorable*, she'd said. Evidently, he'd passed the test with flying colors if she was in on the plan.

Although Naaki was surprised Pat had been able to divert her attention from Ty

Empi Baryeh

long enough to help Thane. As soon as Ty walked into the room, Pat might as well have had her tongue sticking out. She'd practically drooled all over him.

"Did it take a lot of convincing?"

"No." His eyes sparkled with mischief when he grinned. "Once I told her what I had planned, she was happy to help."

"I can't believe she didn't even hint at it."

"I swore her to secrecy."

Naaki sighed deeply, laying her head against Thane's chest. Now that she knew there was no hurry, she could relax and enjoy the airy night, the music, and the man.

ↄↄↄ

Thane retired to his chalet a little after ten, his body charged to the point of frustration. If he didn't do something about it, this was going to be the longest night of his life. He'd done the honorable thing by walking Naaki to her door and leaving her there. The hardest thing he'd ever had to do was kiss her goodnight and walk away. He could still smell her, taste her.

One more second and he'd have thrown all caution to the wind, steered them into the

304

chalet—and her bed. But he didn't want her to feel pressured into doing something she wasn't ready for. Which was why he needed to occupy his mind with anything that could banish thoughts of her and him...and tangled sheets.

His gaze wandered around the room and settled on the well-stocked bar. He had no interest in drinking. He wanted to remember every detail of their date: her radiant smile, the gleam in her gorgeous brown eyes; and when they danced, how her petite form had molded perfectly into him, the feel of her soft breasts pressing against his ribs. He sucked in a jagged breath. His erection pulsed, fighting for release from the fabric restraining it. He groaned. Call him suicidal, but he'd rather be tortured by thoughts of her than try to numb it with alcohol.

He bypassed the drinks, deciding to change out of his dinner clothes and get out his laptop. Work wouldn't take his mind off her, or even douse his arousal, but it would keep him occupied, hopefully tire him out. It was his only hope for getting any kind of sleep tonight.

Entering the bedroom, he didn't glance at the double bed occupying more than half the space. One peek was all it would take to invite a barrage of sensual images of what he'd rather be doing.

He ripped off his bowtie. The damned thing was choking him. The jacket came off next. He tossed both aside and missed the dresser by an inch. He swore and walked over to place them where they should have landed. As he unfastened his cufflinks, his image in the mirror caught his attention. The overhead light was off, leaving the room illuminated by two bedside lamps. They cast a soft golden glow. A completely insane desire to undress Naaki in front of the mirror gripped him. *Dammit, Aleksander, focus.* He whipped around, muttering another curse before hearing a knock on his door.

He frowned. It seemed rather late for anyone to visit, but he welcomed the intrusion. Nothing could kill sexual desire faster than a painfully mundane conversation. He took a moment to compose himself before leaving the room.

He opened the door and caught his breath, because that's exactly what she was...breathtaking. He noticed something more—she looked agitated. *Harassed.* Concern nearly paralyzed him even as he drank in the sight of her. She hadn't changed out of her clothes. Her hair was slightly mussed. Had he done that while kissing her earlier?

"Are you okay?"

Naaki shook her head. "No."

Worry twisted in his chest. She was fine a few minutes ago. What could have happened between then and now? He pulled her into the room, locked the door behind them. He trained his full attention on her while his hand rose to touch her face.

"What can I do to fix it?"

"I think this will help."

Thane's mind didn't fully register what she was doing when she stepped closer. His hand lifted from her face, remaining suspended for a moment. Her breasts grazed his chest as she rose on her tiptoes. He held his breath. Her arms wrapped around his neck, her body flush with his. When their lips touched, he surrendered, taking everything she gave. She held nothing back.

Thane enfolded her in his arms, pulling her even closer, unwilling to let go again. She wiggled. He sucked in a breath.

Their lips parted and their gazes locked as they tried to catch some air.

Her pupils were dilated, the desire in her eyes unmistakable.

"I don't want to say goodnight," she whispered against his lips.

He didn't either, although he probably should. At this point, however, he felt too weak-kneed to walk away. *Oh man.* His heart rammed madly, threatening to break down the walls of his chest. She wasn't actually saying—

"Make love to me, Thane."

It was a sexy command, one he should take advantage of before she changed her mind, yet Thane actually experienced a moment of indecision. "Are you sure about this?"

She withdrew a little. A hint of disappointment crept into her eyes, creating an alluring mélange with the fire of desire still burning in them. "You don't want to be with me?"

He wanted her more than anything else, and to show her how much, he held her waist firm, crushing her abdomen against his rock-hard erection. "Does that feel like I don't want you?"

He felt her tremble. Her fingers dug into his shoulders as she took in a sharp breath. "Then what is it?"

Caressing her cheek, he answered, "Honey, this is a big step. There'll be no turning back after we make love, and I want you to be sure you know what you're asking for."

"I'm sure." Her voice was a sweet melody that had his body humming to its tune.

"Are you?" He searched her face for even a trace of doubt. "I don't take sex lightly. Especially with you—" His voice faltered as he watched her doe eyes flare, her look passionate and trusting—as if she'd have believed anything he told her. It hit him like a revelation, a healing balm reaching to the deepest parts of his being where he still held on to a fear that she was too good to be true. "Naaki, you deserve so much more than I can give."

She pressed a finger on his lips, shutting him up. "Whether now or later, there'll be no turning back. I'm not asking for promises. You're not going to be here forever, which is why we must make the best use of the time we have together." She didn't pause long enough for him to respond before adding, "Love me, Thane."

God knew he already did. And he intended to show her how much. Without any warning, he scooped her up. She let out a surprised cry, which dissolved into a giggle.

He laughed, though the sound echoed with gruff urgency. "Hold on."

Her eyes danced. Her arms tightened around his shoulders. She didn't look away as he advanced towards the bedroom. In front of the dresser, he eased her back to her feet, pausing to gaze at her image in the mirror. The reality was more powerful than anything he could have imagined. The light conspired with the plush furnishing to swathe her honey skin in a veil of shadows. Would he ever be able to uncover all the secrets of her body? Even if he were given a lifetime?

The process of carrying her had pulled down the top she wore, revealing more cleavage. He touched the newly exposed skin, tracing a path along the edge of the dress to her shoulder, and then to the graceful slope of her neck. He loved the feel of her skin.

With little effort, he unhooked her necklace and slipped it into his pocket. Leaning forward, he dropped a feather-light kiss on her nape while his hands sought her zipper.

He raised his eyes to watch her reflection. He didn't want to miss her response.

Her chest rose and fell with her quickening breath. With his heartbeat echoing in his ears, he matched his breathing to hers. The zipper came open, forcing the garment to loosen its embrace. Her skin was warm against his palms as he lifted the top at the waist. She raised her arms, allowing him to ease it up her torso. It caught on her nipples as though intent on teasing him. It worked. The sneak peek at the outer edges of her dark areolas drove him crazy.

He gave the outfit an impatient tug, and his heart soared at the sight of the most exquisite pair of breasts he'd ever seen. They stood firm, rising to dark chocolate peaks that were already beaded.

Once the garment came off, he tossed it on the dresser next to his jacket and returned his eager attention to her equally eager breasts. He cupped them, and just as he'd imagined so many times before, they fit into his hands perfectly.

"Ahh, lovely," he whispered into her ear.

She responded with a moan and leaned back into him. Her nipples hardened further beneath his palms. It sent his body into overdrive. However, he was determined to take it slowly, not only to give her ample time to change her mind, but he knew without that control he might not last long enough to take her with him. He wanted to watch her pleasure, watch her shudder and moan, and know he'd made her feel every bit as incredible as she made him feel.

Her hands covered his as he gently kneaded her breasts. Did she have any idea how erotic he found the gesture, how it had him grappling with his last vestige of restraint? He withdrew his hands from her chest, absorbing the feel of her silken skin as he skimmed it to the back of her skirt. He groped in search of a zipper or button.

"It's on the side." The thick-with-desire voice spoke to his mounting need and made him groan. He found the zipper and pulled hard, nearly ripping the pull in his impatience. He released the soft fabric and allowed it to fall in a pool at her feet. He exhaled through his mouth; he couldn't help staring. Underneath the skirt, she wore black lacey panties. Even sexier than that, was a colorful set of stringed beads around her hips sitting on the top of the flimsy fabric like a rainbow cradling her womanhood. His breath whooshed out of his lungs as if he'd been kicked in the gut. Losing a measure of control, he grabbed her by the shoulders and turned her around.

He captured her mouth with his, urgently probing and seeking, coaxing and stroking. She allowed him entry, and he savored her warm mouth with his tongue. Her noises drove him wild. The kiss deepened as she met him with equal passion until they had to catch their breaths.

"My sweet Naaki," he whispered as he met her gaze briefly before finding her lips again.

❧❧❧

Naaki melted into him, moaning as hot sensations swirled below her navel. Her hands traveled across his solid chest, absorbing the heat of his body as it radiated through his shirt. She wanted it off. Her hands frantically sought his top button. The blasted thing wouldn't come off. Her frustration must have shown since Thane's hand closed over hers in a firm grip that halted her fumbling attempt to undress him.

He broke the kiss to look at her. His lips curved up in a smile; hers parted. She was hungry to taste him again.

"What do you want?" he asked.

*Everything.* "I want this off."

"As you wish." He seized the collars of his shirt and ripped it open.

Naaki's eyes widened. Thane ripping his shirt open was definitely one of the sexiest things on earth. She was aware of the eagerness he tried hard to conceal, but she hadn't expected *that*. He released a deep chuckle.

"Snaps," he explained, shrugging off the shirt.

"Good." She had no time to worry about the shirt, anyway. She was too busy feasting her eyes on his bare chest. She ran her palms through the velvety hair, using the gesture to mask the trembling of her hands. The heat from his body consumed her. Control didn't come easily, especially since she was completely conscious of his watchful stare at her near nakedness in the mirror. She wasn't shy, though. Rather, the hunger and appreciation in his eyes made her feel incredibly sexy. Seeing the effect she had on him, emboldened her.

"The trousers too."

CHANCING FAITH

Obediently, he reached for his belt and started unbuckling. The parts of her skin where his hands had just been felt suddenly cold and exposed. She couldn't wait for him to resume his devastating caresses. Her eyes were riveted on him as he took off the pants. Then he was standing before her, his underwear sporting a virile testimony to his arousal.

Her breath hiked. "I want to see you."

Her heart raced as he slipped the briefs down to his knees and used his leg to take them the rest of the way. As he raised himself, his erection bumped into her stomach. All the tingles she'd experienced before paled in comparison to the sharp sensation that pierced her, turning her legs to jelly. Luckily his arms were there to hold her. She gave up her lips to another kiss, sighing contentedly as his tongue masterfully mated with hers. He cupped her butt, grinding his hips into her stomach. Liquid heat curled in her center as she continued to pulse with need.

She was unaware of moving until her calves came into contact with the bed. Her knees gave way and she tumbled backwards. Her mind only half-registered the soft comfort surrounding her but was acutely aware of the man now towering over her. He knelt astride her, then leaning in he hooked his thumbs into her panties and peeled them off. He paused to gaze at her nakedness. She trembled under his appreciative stare, yearning for more of his touch.

He bent over her, propping himself on both hands and every coherent word flew out of her mind.

"Touch me," he whispered.

Her hands journeyed over his smooth skin, learning the hard planes of the body of the man she loved. Moving downwards, she found his engorged member. Her fingers ran lovingly along the length of it before encircling him. He felt glorious—warm, silken, hard, pulsing. She tightened her grip and he closed his eyes, releasing a harsh breath. The ache in her core intensified.

He weaved his fingers through her femininity beads, rolling them over her stomach. It was a new sensation that only made her yearn for more. He seemed to know exactly what to do to drive her crazy. She parted her legs, letting him know where his attention was needed. Only his touch would relieve her mounting desire. Without hesitation, his hand moved down finding her heat. She whimpered as intense pleasure racked her body. Then he entered her with his finger. Her hips rocked forward, needing more of his brand of pain relief. His intimate stroking brought a brief measure of satisfaction before her yearning escalated.

"Thane." His name tumbled out of her throat once, twice, and again.

He answered each time, but she couldn't find the words to tell him. All she could do was give herself completely to him, allowing him to work his expert hands on her with the precision and artistry of a potter molding delicate clay with love. He lowered himself onto her, capturing one nipple in his mouth. She bit her lip, barely able to contain the double dose of pleasure. After a moment, he moved his attention to the other nipple, leaving the first one cool, the second hot. The contrast had her writhing under him, wanting more of the titillating sensations consuming her.

"Thane, I need you," she hissed urgently. "I want everything."

Without leaving her heat, he reached his other hand somewhere above her head and produced a condom. Ripping it with his teeth, he sheathed himself. Her breath came in rapid bursts in anticipation of his eventual entry. He angled her sideways, prodded her legs further apart with his knee. He curled a hand under her thigh, sliding her leg up to his hip until his hot, hard tip nudged her slick opening.

His face hovered just inches away from hers as he began to fill her. Her abdomen tightened. She tried not to flinch, or tense up, afraid he might sense her inexperience and stop. She didn't want to stop, didn't want to leave his warm embrace. As he met her body's resistance, she gripped him. *Relax*, she told herself, remembering her best friend's advice.

"Kiss me," she whispered thickly.

And he did. A sigh left her lips, disappearing into his mouth in a long moan until she was only aware of his exquisite taste and the multitude of sensations building up inside her. Her body's resistance gave way as he slowly sank into her.

"God...Naaki, you feel so good." The sound of his strained voice reached down to her soul. A sense of completeness enveloped her and she knew without a doubt she was totally and unconditionally his. He paused for a second, letting her get used to his size. "Are you all right?"

She nodded, since words were suddenly not part of her reality. Melding the length of his body to hers, he began to move inside her. She shuddered, welcoming the onslaught of emotions bombarding her body as they found their rhythm. Each time they came together, she trembled. Her arms encircled him, her fingers dug into his hair. She moaned his name just before he found her lips.

His groans mixed with hers as the deep, deliberate rhythm of their love-making quickened. Her body became taut. Her universe turned on its axis. She held on to him, afraid she'd drift away if she let go. She rocked against him, taking him deeper, soaring higher as he whispered endearments into her ear. Then he began to stroke her nipple and that additional touch set off a time bomb. She cried out as a guttural groan erupted from him, then she exploded into a million pieces.

Her release came in waves, shaking her until she finally became limp, sated. His gray eyes were the first things she saw when she reopened hers as she floated back to earth. Her pulse continued to race. The only sound that could be heard was their breathing.

# CHAPTER 17

Thane awoke with a sense of completeness. It had everything to do with the woman sleeping in his arms. He pulled her closer into the spoon they'd settled into after making love last night. In the quiet pre-dawn hour, he was aware of nothing other than her soft feminine form snuggled up against him. He took a long drag of the morning air, savoring its crisp freshness mingled with Naaki's wild herb smell. For the first time in a long time, he felt no rush to get out of bed, no urgency to check his email or monitor the stock market. He wanted to spend the rest of the day in bed, making love with Naaki.

Funny, he'd thought loving her meant risking his heart, yet listening to her gentle breathing he knew entrusting her with his heart was the best decision he'd ever made. If only he'd known this a couple of weeks ago. His breath caught as emotions consumed him. His hand ran lazily along the length of her arm as the memory of those arms wrapped around him spilled into his thoughts. He inclined his head and placed a gentle kiss on her exposed shoulder.

She stirred, wiggled her hips and settled in a more comfortable position—one that brought his morning arousal scandalously close to her womanhood. Instant heat flamed his body. A contented sigh left her lips while he groaned as pressure built up in his groin. He cupped his hand over her breast, tucking his fingers between her and the bed. His thumb caressed her skin.

The corners of his lips edged upwards when she moaned. Another kiss dropped on her nape and bolder hand strokes had her heart racing. He could feel her pulse against the tips of his fingers as though he was holding her heart in his hand.

He intended to treasure it.

Another soft moan from her emboldened him. He moved the hand covering her breast, feeling the tightening of her nipple. She stirred and her hand rose, overlaying his. Her fingers slipped between his and squeezed gently. He knew she was awake before she turned around. She looked replete...beautiful.

A lazy smile formed on her lips as their stares met. "Hi," she said.

For a moment, Thane didn't respond. A rush of emotions surged forward, overwhelming him. His throat tightened. He swallowed.

"This look suits you," he eventually managed.

"What look?" Her voice was soft as silk, her eyes expectant, already fully waked.

"Relaxed, sated. We'll just call it the afterglow." He gave her a lingering kiss, slipping two fingers through her beads. He grazed the skin beneath—that, among many others, was one of the sensitive spots he'd discovered last night. She trembled, catching her breath. Drawing back, Thane continued to play with the beads. "I like these."

Her lips parted with the beginning of a response, but it turned into a gasp as he applied pressure to his touch. Her fingers dug into his shoulder. Her eyes began to cloud with desire.

"Sexy," he rasped, releasing her beads to seek her breasts.

She raised her hand and touched his face, her fingers tracing his features in a gesture so tender, his heart shuddered.

"I love you." The words tumbled out without warning and he realized he wanted her to know.

The rise and fall of her chest stopped for a moment, and when it returned her breath came in more rapid bursts. The affection— and want—intensified in her eyes. "I love you, too."

He'd already seen it in her expression, but actually hearing her say the words weakened him, although he'd never felt more secure. A need to promise her a life together gripped him. The words rose to the tip of his tongue, threatening to spill out. He forced them back. It was too much pressure to lay on her when he knew their ambitions would likely take them on separate paths, shattering any hopes of forever. He swallowed the sudden overpowering need to bury his face in the crook of her neck and weep.

Instead, he kissed her. Through his actions, he would show her what he couldn't say—that his heart belonged to her forever.

⋐⋑⋐⋑

They ordered room service and spent the rest of the morning in bed, finally emerging from the chalet well into the afternoon, swathed in the blissful aftermath of their love-making. They found a guide to give them a tour of the grounds. Like a newlywed, Thane had a hard time keeping his hands off Naaki as they explored the garden's exotic vegetation. In the evening, they had a less formal dinner at the gazebo and retired to Naaki's chalet for the night.

By Sunday evening, Thane was fairly certain he'd done what he'd resolved to do—show her in every non-verbal way he knew that he was hers. They'd spent the day wrapped up in each other, refusing to acknowledge that their weekend escape would be ending in a few hours.

The drive back to Accra was quiet, although his free hand was linked with hers, and their gazes met for a couple of seconds every few minutes. Each time she smiled, he had to resist the urge to turn around and go back to the gardens.

On the outskirts of the city, Thane switched on his cell phone. The device beeped several times with backed-up messages. Boy was he glad he'd turned it off for the weekend. A quick check showed that most of the missed calls were from Steven Black.

He really didn't want to deal with Steve right now. His preferred plan was to go home with Naaki and spend the night with her, but he knew a wiser move was to go to *his* home and catch up on work before tomorrow morning—starting with a call to Black & Black's CEO to find out what was so damned important to warrant his multiple messages.

He dropped Naaki off and did what he realized would never get easier no matter how many times they made love—kiss her goodbye and walk away.

❦❦

Naaki giggled as wanton thrills swamped her. She hadn't been able to stop grinning as she drove to work the next morning, consumed with anticipation at the prospect of seeing Thane today. She must have looked like an idiot, judging by the curious glance a driver in the opposite lane threw her. She was too happy to care. Her hands tightened around the steering wheel, tingling at the memory of exploring Thane's sculpted body. It was hard to believe she'd been in his arms less than twenty-four hours ago.

She missed him already.

Not that she'd expected otherwise. She'd started missing him the moment they reached the outskirts of town and his cell phone began beeping. Though he'd pretended to ignore them—for her sake, she was sure—she couldn't help noticing the measured look, the same one he often sported in the office. He'd started slipping into "business mode." She'd invited him to stay the night, anyway, hoping he'd get work out of the way quickly so they could pick up where they left off in Aburi.

Naaki smiled at the driver in the next lane, although her mind was elsewhere, remembering Thane's response to the invitation. He'd pulled her into his arms and kissed her, slowly and passionately, melting her right at her doorstep. He'd then told her if he didn't leave, work would be the last thing on his mind. He had, however, accepted an invitation for tea and they'd ended up making love on her kitchen counter. Sated, yet still wanting him, she'd cradled him close to her heart as the minutes ticked away. With a final kiss he'd driven off, promising her to-night.

Naaki couldn't wait. She'd started counting the minutes as soon as his taillights disappeared from view.

By the time she parked her car in front of the office building she was buzzing with energy, riding on a new high, her heart pulsating exuberantly. Just like last night. Her mind had refused to shut down, preferring to relive her weekend with Thane in vivid detail. It was hours after midnight that her body, too exhausted from all her exertions, had succeeded in subduing her supercharged mind.

She stepped out of the car and took a moment to compose herself. It wouldn't do to appear distracted when her colleagues expected her to be on the ball. She checked her time. Seven-fifty. She usually got in at least twenty minutes before eight so she could check mail and plan her day before meetings and client calls inevitably began. By her standards, she was late, and last Friday being a holiday, every client would be checking in on their projects. With all that in mind, she knew there was no time to see Thane before work started. Besides, she hadn't noticed his car outside, so he was probably starting his day at a client's.

At the reception, she offered a hearty greeting to Aku, but didn't stop to chat like she usually did. When she walked into the office, most of her colleagues were at their desks staring intently at their computers. The exception was Grace who was yelling at someone on the other end of a phone conversation. No surprises there.

Naaki smiled, making her way to her desk. At least it didn't appear to be a crazy Monday morning. That assessment held true for most of the morning while she sorted out emails, checked the status of her projects in the creative studio, updated clients and attended the weekly account executives meeting. Shortly after eleven o'clock, Mr. Boateng's personal assistant came to announce an emergency meeting and all hell broke loose.

Normally upbeat and full of energy, Joe's manner was stiff as he announced all staff must convene in the boardroom immediately. Naaki noted he didn't make eye contact with anyone. A sliver of concern sneaked into her, coiling around her insides. She shook herself. Joe probably just had a bad weekend.

And just like that the worry vanished, replaced with an onrush of that delectable, silken sensation which came with thinking about Thane. She concealed her smile as she put her computer on standby and filed out with the rest of the team.

ののの

The murmur of several pockets of conversation filled the boardroom. Naaki didn't join in. She assumed a false calmness, knowing she needed that pretense of composure when Thane walked in any moment from now. She hadn't worked out how she'd act around him at work. Would they be open about their relationship? Would members of the team feel threatened?

As an intern, she wasn't exactly in competition with them. Even if she were, Thane had proven convincingly that he was impartial. Besides, in a few months she'd be out of there and it wouldn't matter. Funny how those concerns seemed insurmountable a couple of weeks ago but now felt like mere details—details that could be worked out.

Conversations ceased when the door opened and a grim-faced Mr. Boateng stepped in. Without Thane, Naaki noted. She also noticed he wasn't wearing a tie. The look was a far cry from his usual sharp appearance, giving Naaki the impression that the tie had been yanked off moments earlier.

Mr. Boateng rested his hands on his rotund waist. "Team—"

That one word spoken in a voice lacking any hint of buoyancy sent a chill down Naaki's spine. It was a feeling she'd felt only once before—when her father had arrived home one October afternoon two years ago and announced the passing away of his twin sister who'd been in a serious accident a week before. He'd returned home from the hospital, his eyes devoid of their usual luster. He'd shaken his head and she'd known then, as she did now, that something was terribly wrong.

She clasped her hand together, making a conscious effort to keep taking deep breaths.

"We've just received an email—" Mr. Boateng paused again, shaking his head as though he didn't want to believe what he was about to say. "Black & Black has dropped out of the negotiations. We're on our own."

Was it just her or had the room temperature suddenly dropped? No one spoke for a moment as the silent echo of the managing director's words sank in.

Grace was the first recover. "What are you saying, sir?"

Naaki had that question and more. Why, being at the top of the list. Had MIA done anything in the past few weeks to cause Black & Black to lose interest? Where did that leave the agency? Her internship?

And Thane? Where did that leave her and Thane?

Her heart kicked. No deal meant he had no reason to stay. They'd agreed to be together until he returned to America. Worry coiled around her insides, seizing control of her hands, which were still firmly clasped together. Her throat tightened, causing her breathing to falter. She wasn't ready to say goodbye, wasn't ready for her heart to break as she knew it would when he left.

"They sent an email?" A voice, sounding incredulous, broke through the barrage of her thoughts. "Is that ethical?"

"They needed it on record," another stunned voice said.

Naaki was only partially attentive to the speculative questions. While they were all important and certainly needed to be asked, only one thing mattered to her. Whatever was wrong, whatever MIA's fault, Thane could fix it. He had to.

"D—Does Thane know?" Her voice was shaky, barely audible.

Someone echoed her question loud enough for everyone to hear.

"Where *is* Thane?" another followed.

Mr. Boateng didn't answer immediately. His grim look was now replaced by one of schooled diplomacy. Naaki held on to that, willing herself to believe things weren't as bad as she was tempted to think. Until Mr. Boateng's next words shattered her completely.

"By now—" He briefly diverted his attention to the conference room clock, "—he's air-bound, halfway between Ghana and the United States."

Naaki didn't hear any more. Her heart jolted. The emotions rushed in all at once, slamming into her with a force that left her unprepared and exposed. Internally, she could feel herself shaking. Outwardly—

She didn't care what she looked like outwardly. Not when her insides were ripping apart, bit by excruciating bit. He was gone. After pulling off the most romantic weekend getaway, after giving her the best three days of her life...after saying he loved her. They'd spent a whole weekend making love. He'd promised her tonight. And now he was...gone? *Without saying goodbye.*

Now she saw it clearly, how he'd manipulated her naïve heart, carefully wooed her, laid the bait and patiently waited for her to fall. She'd been easy prey, absorbing the attention he gave in her desperate need for affirmation. She refused to dwell on the shock and hurt of realizing Thane had used her, after all.

She had no idea how she did it, but somehow she managed to sit through the rest of the meeting while they discussed the next step for MIA. She even pitched in as they developed a crisis plan. They would need it, since the anticipated association with Black & Black had been a strong selling point in signing on their newly acquired clients.

Thankfully she managed to hold herself together till the end of the meeting.

When Mr. Boateng dismissed them, she breathed relief. Now she could find somewhere to hide and let out the barely held back tears.

"Hold on, Naaki," Mr. Boateng called.

She tried to hide her disappointment, avoiding his gaze so he wouldn't see she was holding herself together by a thread. Any moment now she'd fall apart. She hoped it wouldn't be in front of anyone.

When they were alone, Mr. Boateng turned to face her. "You don't have to go through this, Naaki. You have your professional certification to think of." The fatherly concern in his voice nearly undid her. "I've been speaking to the coordinator at CIM to have you reassigned."

"I—" She didn't know what to say. This wasn't how she'd imagined the end of her attachment. She wanted to stay, to help, but she also needed to complete her internship. The decision to stay or leave was one she didn't fully trust herself to make right away.

"For now, though, I hate to ask but I need you to attend a meeting at The Mobile Company," he continued, saving her the trouble of finding an appropriate response. "I understand you pitched that account. Kevin will go with you so he can take over once we find a new place for you to complete your internship."

Her throat tightened. The mention of the TMC pitch was like a slash to her already bleeding heart. Thane had been there all the way. She remembered the exhilaration of that triumphant moment when she completed the presentation...Thane's praise, lunch to celebrate. It all came back, bittersweet and harrowing.

"Yes, sir."

She waited for him to leave before sinking onto one of the chairs. Elbows on the table, she buried her face in her palms. A small cry rose from deep within her soul, and gradually the tears came.

# CHAPTER 18

Thane stared at the phone, seething. He'd just gotten off a call with Steven Black, and his brother, Leo. How he'd managed to work with the brothers for over five years was a wonder. Steve and Leo were assholes—he'd always known that—but this latest stunt was a low blow even for them.

Sunday was the first he'd heard about Black & Black's decision to quit the negotiations with MIA. It hadn't been a discussion. Since Thane had been unavailable all weekend, they'd gone ahead and made their decision. Unbeknown to him, they'd been in talks with a Nigerian agency as if they'd doubted his ability to get Black & Black the best deal with MIA.

Rage consumed him, seeking an avenue for release. He wasn't a violent person, but right this minute he'd have loved nothing better than to break Steve's nose with his fist. He swore, flexing his fingers to work out the anger building up within. It was the second time in his life he'd been blindsided like this.

Decisions of that magnitude weren't made on a whim. The excuse of him being unavailable over the weekend was just that— an excuse. The question was, had this been the plan all along or had the new opportunity presented itself to the brothers after he'd left for Ghana?

He shook his head. Either way they could have waited, kept him in the loop.

Instead, they'd had the audacity to book him on a flight out of Ghana for Monday morning and order him back with no time to regain his bearings. Disoriented by the entire scenario, he'd packed his bags, intending to return home as instructed, and, there, personally make a case for MIA.

He'd gone as far as the boarding gate, and then realized he couldn't leave, couldn't sneak out like a con artist and let MIA face the consequences alone. He couldn't do it to Naaki.

His heart lurched. *Naaki.*

He hoped she'd understand why he hadn't contacted her in the past three days. She was all he could think about, yet it was imperative he remained focused on the task at hand. He needed to be level-headed while negotiating what could possibly be the most important deal of his life.

A few weeks ago, his single-minded objective had been to complete the negotiations with MIA. It was supposed to be the clincher in his petition for partner.

Now he was sure he didn't need Black & Black. While standing with his passport in hand, listening to the final boarding call and wishing like hell his heart would stop ripping to bits, he'd realized he needed Naaki more than he'd needed anything—any*one*—before.

Ty's voice reeled him fully back to the present. "Staring at the phone isn't going to make it ring, you know."

They were in Thane's living room going over Ty's financial report, which was initially to go to Black & Black. Now Thane had another plan. Since he was still technically with the American agency, he had every right to review the details of the report.

338

Ty had agreed to hold the information for twenty-four hours. It was all the time Thane needed, because by close of day his association with Black & Black would be over and he would be the new fifty-one percent owner of MIA. He would be able to stop the information from ever getting to Black & Black.

Thane huffed, ignoring the obvious sarcasm in Ty's tone. "This thing has got to come together today. The longer it takes—"

*The harder the separation from Naaki will be.* Thane wasn't sure he could take another day of not hearing her voice. He didn't want to go there, though, so he said, "I don't like this...waiting on other people."

Already, several factors were acting to increase his nervousness. The fact of relocating to Ghana coupled with the shift from employee to business owner ranked high on the list.

Walking over to one window, he shoved one hand into his pocket as the other reached up to rub his neck. He'd barely slept the past couple of days as he called in favors to find out all he could about the Nigerian agency Black & Black was in negotiations with. His initial research had revealed some disturbing information—disturbing for Black & Black, that is. He was waiting for confirmation of his suspicions that the Nigerian agency didn't have nearly the kind of clout or sub-regional respect MIA still commanded.

Once Steve and Leo discovered this, they'd want to resume talks with MIA. When they did, Thane wouldn't be interested. This made it imperative that everything was settled today. The longer it took, the greater the chances of the Blacks discovering the truth about their Nigerian business interest—and Thane's personal interest in MIA.

If by that time, his association with Black & Black hadn't been severed, his plans could fall through. He'd lose everything.

Ty came to stand next to him. "You've done your part. You've got to trust that. None of those we're waiting on stands to gain from not coming through."

Thane took in a deep breath, nodding. "You're right." He was dealing with people he'd worked with before and trusted, most of whom actually stood to benefit from this new setup.

A moment of thoughtful silence passed before Ty spoke again. "That's not the only thing on your mind, though, is it?"

A whisper of uneasiness settled in Thane's chest. He kept his gaze on the sunny scenes outside, though he wasn't particularly focused on anything. His stomach tightened uncomfortably. "I'm doing the right thing," he said more for himself than his friend.

"You're not having second thoughts?"

Thane pocketed his other hand. "No, of course not."

He didn't need to think about it. When he'd decided not to board the plane on Monday, he made his choice. Naaki. If he had to stay here to be with her, that was what he'd do. Nothing else mattered. The fact that MIA provided a viable investment for him was a bonus.

"I love this country." What he really meant was he loved Naaki—the reason why the note of unease persisted.

How would she take the news? Would she feel pressured? More importantly, how was she handling the silence he'd imposed on her without prior notice? He cursed. "I should have called her."

Ty tapped his shoulder briefly as though making sure he had Thane's attention. "It's never too late. Besides, one glance at how miserable you look and she'll have to forgive you."

This time Thane turned. Seeing the grin on Ty's face, he scowled even though his insides roiled with renewed anticipation. He was grateful to Ty for trying to lighten the mood, but he couldn't come up with an equally jovial reply.

Still smiling, Ty said, "Chances are she's just as miserable."

And it would be his fault. Before Thane could respond, the sound of his cell phone ringing interrupted them.

"Finally," he murmured, refocusing his mind as he hastened back to the table to answer it.

ℰℐℰℐ

The steam had stopped rising from the tea. Naaki stared into the liquid, drowning in memories of Thane. She touched the countertop, remembering the last time they'd made love. Her lips began to quiver and her heart contorted as if something was trying to snuff the life out of her. Three days after receiving the shocking news of Thane's betrayal, the pain hadn't subsided. How was it possible for her heart to break anew every day?

The heartache and loneliness were easier to handle at work, because there was so much to do to manage the crisis situation. At home, however, she had no protection. How did she dispel thoughts of someone who had become intertwined with everything she cherished: work, home, tea time...her heart?

Somehow she summoned enough will-power to prevent herself from crying again. In time the thoughts would fade to a faraway memory. At least her mother and Pat promised as much. She wasn't sure the pain could ever fade, but she focused on the possibility. Perhaps if she did it enough times, she'd begin to believe it. Picking up the mug, she dumped its content into the sink without tasting it.

She decided to call Pat and invite her over. She could use the company of her best friend tonight. She left the kitchen, remembering only then she'd actually gone in there to start supper. She shrugged. It could wait.

As she crossed the corridor, heading towards the living room where she'd left her handbag, she heard a knock on her front door. The unexpected sound made her jump, stirring an unwarranted thrill. It died away just as quickly as she reminded herself Thane couldn't possibly be the one outside her door.

Nevertheless, a scintilla of that illogical feeling lingered. She hurried to unlock the door, jerking it open. Hope crumpled as she recognized Gyamfi through the screen door. Her first instinct was to slam the door shut, but she realized that wouldn't make her feel better. Taking in a deep, calming breath, she opened the screen door as well.

Gyamfi stared back at her as though waiting for her to speak first.

She didn't.

"Are you going to invite me in?"

Naaki wondered why it seemed such an odd question until she remembered he usually just barreled in. She took in his appearance. He wore one of his trademark power suits, his tie still looking neat even though the working day had ended more than two hours ago. She couldn't help thinking he looked snooty. Nothing like Thane who gave a whole new meaning to tailor-made when he wore a suit. Or maybe her assessment had to do with the fact that she knew both men.

Her insides twisted as she reminded herself she hadn't really known Thane at all.

"What do you want?"

"You aren't going to make me stand out here on your porch, are you?" When she didn't make a move to invite him in, he had the grace to look embarrassed. "Can we talk?"

She considered his question for a moment before stepping aside for him to enter.

"It won't take more than five minutes," he assured her.

"Good, because I have plans." The earlier she let him say what he came here to tell her, the sooner he'd be out of here. Besides, standing there with her doors open was an open invitation to mosquitoes.

She shut the screen door but left the main one open to show him she expected this to be a "walk-in, walk-out" visit. In the living room, he refused her offer of a seat, which was just as well. She didn't offer anything else. Water was culturally required as a welcome sign to a guest, but she wanted to make doubly sure Gyamfi knew the sentiment didn't apply to him.

"What did you want to talk about?"

"Us."

Empi Baryeh

She began to refute the notion of there being an "us," but he held up a hand. "Hear me out, please."

Naaki was too stunned to speak. In Gyamfi parlance, "please" amounted to begging—something he usually didn't do.

"I've been thinking..." He hesitated. "My mother and I have been talking." He paused again. "She really misses you."

"You seriously came all this way to tell me this?"

"Yes—" He made a face. "No, of course not."

"Then what?"

"I made a mistake letting you go," he said. "When you broke up with me, you said some things—"

"I remember what I said, Gyamfi. I meant them."

"I didn't take it well."

She scoffed. "That's an interesting way of putting it."

He'd been livid about her wanting a career so much that she'd give him up. All she'd wanted—still wanted—was someone who respected her mind enough to support her dreams, someone who couldn't imagine his life without her. Gyamfi had expected her

346

to give up her ambitions in exchange for him taking care of her and their future children.

"All right," he conceded. "My point is, I've had time to think about it. I want you in my life. My mother approves of you, and if you want to work—" He threw his hands up in a gesture of concession. He actually looked uncomfortable. It made Naaki wonder if he was doing this for himself or his mother. "There are many things you can do, aside from advertising, and still take care of our home."

Naaki laughed though she really wanted to cry. Even in his compromise, he wanted to dictate what she could do.

"I have a lot of connections—" he started to say again.

"Stop. Please."

He stared at her, taken aback.

Naaki felt something she never expected to feel towards him. Pity. "Can't you see this won't work? We're not on the same page. I need to pursue my own dreams and I'm sure you'll soon meet someone who feels—"

"I want you!"

It was her turn to be blown out of the water. "I don't want you, Gyamfi. I don't love you."

His eyes narrowed, shooting darts of suspicion her way. "Is this about that American?"

Yes and no. Gyamfi had ceased to be her man of choice even before Thane came along and more so now that she'd had a taste of what she really wanted.

"His name is Thane," she said. "You need to leave."

He didn't. Instead, he continued to stare at her as if trying to decipher some secret. "You've slept with him."

It was an accusation—one that pierced her already shattered heart, leaving her unprepared.

Gyamfi cursed. "You don't deny it this time."

She raised her chin up and squared her shoulders. "I don't answer to you."

His look became thunderous. "I waited for you! I respected you because I thought you were a lady." He closed the space between them in two steps, pinning her against the wall. "But since you've already started spreading your legs..." He let his words hang.

Trapped. Naaki couldn't move. Panic gripped her, but she was determined not to show it. '*Imagine yourself in an open space and breathe.*' Thane's words, spoken a few weeks ago, spilled into her mind, infusing her with strength. She needed to concentrate on something other than the feeling of being confined. As she focused her mind, the fear began to subside and she realized she could move one hand. She jabbed him in the ribs but it didn't seem to do any damage.

Stunned tears flowed down her face unrestrained. "Gyamfi, let go." She wouldn't give him the satisfaction of begging.

He gripped her jaw firmly, forcing her face up. "I'm going to show you what you've been missing."

She screamed, struggling to escape his grip. Suddenly her leg came free and she jerked her knee. Hard. He released her immediately, shrieking in pain and anger. She saw his hand go up. He was about to strike her when someone pulled him off her. Naaki's hands immediately rose to her jaw, which hurt from his iron grip. Without wasting time to check who her rescuer was, she looked around for something. A weapon. Her gaze fell on a bottle of wine that had been sitting on her living room sideboard since the weekend trip back from Aburi. She grabbed it and turned in time to see Gyamfi's crashing onto the floor and Thane advancing toward him, fists closed.

She stood transfixed. *Thane?*

Gyamfi scrambled to his feet before Thane could floor him again. He swung at Thane and missed. His mistake, because Thane seized him by the collar and landed another blow. Gyamfi lifted his hands in surrender as Thane raised his fist again.

"Get out!" Thane growled, throwing Gyamfi away from him.

Gyamfi staggered backwards a few steps before regaining his balance. His lip was split and blood trickled from his nostrils. He sniffed, producing a handkerchief from his pocket. He wiped at the blood and dabbed the split on his lip. He shot a dirty look at Naaki over Thane's shoulder. She raised the bottle, emboldened.

Gyamfi's gaze returned to Thane who still stood with a menacing stance.

"Leave, Gyamfi," Naaki said, stepping forward. "You're no longer welcome in my house."

Thane caught her arm and pulled her back, putting himself between her and Gyamfi.

Gyamfi threw her one last foul look before turning to Thane. "You can have her. She's already used merchandise anyway." With that, he stomped out.

It wasn't until the door slammed shut that Naaki allowed herself to fathom what had just happened, the magnitude of what Gyamfi had been about to do, Thane coming to her rescue.

"Are you okay?" he asked, turning her to face him.

She nodded. "He was going to—" Her hands began to shake. The maelstrom of emotions she'd tried to hold at bay earlier all came crashing back. This time she couldn't stop herself from crying.

Thane took the bottle from her shaky hands, replacing it on the sideboard before enveloping her in his arms. "Shh, I'm here now. I won't let him hurt you."

She sank into his embrace, clutching his shirt as if he'd disappear again if she didn't. Soon she realized she had to stop needing him. She mustered enough courage to pull back, but his arms prevented her from completely withdrawing from his warm embrace.

She gazed up into his familiar gray eyes. "Are you real?" Despite touching him, feeling his breath against her face, she needed to hear it from him.

"I am."

A healing wave began to pulse through her, but she refused to acknowledge it. If she'd learned anything from the past three days, it was that she couldn't afford to get attached to Thane again. She wouldn't survive the next time he left. She drew back, this time completely disentangling herself from his arms. He didn't attempt to pull her back.

"When did you come back?" How long did he plan on staying? When would her heart start breaking again?

"I never left."

"You didn't?" She frowned. If he didn't leave, then how come she hadn't heard from him in three days? Was she that forgettable? "Mr. Boateng said—"

"Black & Black made the decision without me," he cut in. "Everything was set, my return flight booked. I thought the only way to change their minds was in person, but after reaching the airport I realized I only had one real choice." He took a step closer, and she took one back. "Naaki—"

"You can't waltz in and bring hope to people just to take it away again, Thane."

She fought to keep her emotions in check. "We trusted you. *I* trusted you."

The spark in his eyes dimmed a notch as he let out a heavy breath. She noticed the tired rings around his eyes. He looked as if he hadn't had much sleep since the last time she saw him. Her stomach knotted in several places. She wanted to reach out and touch him, but she was afraid doing so would only make it harder to let him go.

"I know," he said. "That's why I couldn't leave. When I made up my mind not to board the plane, I knew I had to come up with a plan to fix the situation. I thought if I focused on it, I'd be able to help us fight Black & Black."

"You're too late—"

He didn't let her finish. "No. It can't be too late."

He reached her with two steps and placed his hands on her shoulders. His touch was loose enough for her to shrug off, but she didn't. She needed to absorb enough of him to keep her going after he left again.

"I need you. I love you."

"I meant it's too late for you to help MIA," she clarified. "There's a new owner. I guess someone believed in the agency a little more than you did."

He took her hands. "Not someone, Naaki. Me." For the first time this evening, he smiled. It was a slight one but it turned her insides to mush. "I'm the one who believes in MIA."

Naaki gaped at him, silent. Obviously, she hadn't heard correctly.

"It's what I've been doing the past three days."

Finally, she began to understand why he'd stayed away—not because he'd gotten what he wanted from her. He'd done it to save the agency. "What about Black & Black?"

"I don't work for them anymore." He brought her hands to his lips and pressed a gentle kiss on her fingers, sending a shiver down her spine. "Do you remember when you told me about your dream of marketing Ghana as a tourist destination?"

She nodded.

"I want to be part of your dream, if you'll let me. I have the resources, MIA has the regional network, and you..." He gazed into her eyes, his look warm and hopeful. "You have the passion."

"What about you? Your ambition?"

"I can make a name for myself right here. My heart is invested in you and this country. I'm not going anywhere unless you're coming with me."

The tears that filled her eyes now weren't those of sorrow.

"The past three days without you have been miserable," he continued. "I should have called and shared my plans with you. I promise I'll never keep anything from you again. I need you, Naaki. Forgive me for hurting you."

She smiled through her tears, her heart overflowing with love. "I forgive you."

He pulled her closer and she went willingly, draping her arms over his broad shoulders.

"I forgive you," she whispered again.

"I love you."

She gazed up at him with total and complete affection. "I love you."

His eyes misted as though she'd finally said the one thing he'd been waiting to hear. He cupped her face and kissed her. This was what she'd wanted to do since he swooped in and rescued her. Standing on tiptoes, she kissed him back, holding nothing in.

Thane pulled away, breathing hard. "Do you have plans tonight?"

"I was going to ask Pat over."

"Good thing I'm here, then. She's on a date with Ty."

Naaki gasped. Good news really did come in multiples. "Ty and Pat?"

"He's enthralled with her, as I am with you." His eyes held a mischievous gleam. "Now where were we?"

"You were showing me how much you missed me."

He chuckled. "Ah, yes, but before we continue, I need to ask you something."

"What?" She beamed. He could ask anything as long as he followed it with one of his toe-curling kisses.

"What's the proper way to ask you to marry me?"

She sniffed as fresh tears welled up her eyes "Are you asking me to—"

"Yes, Naaki Faith Tabika. I'm asking you to do me the honor of becoming my wife...if you have room for one more in your life," he answered.

Naaki sniffed again. Marriage had been something she hoped for in the distant future, after her career was established—and if she found someone willing support her dreams. In Thane she discovered she could have both right now. Loving him didn't mean losing herself, and she didn't want to wait till some unknown future date to marry him.

"I do with all my heart." She leaned in for a kiss.

"Now let's get back to me showing you how much I missed you," he said, sweeping off her feet—literally.

## THE END

# About the Author

Empi Baryeh has been writing since the age of thirteen after stumbling upon a YA story her older sister had started. The story fascinated her so much that, when she discovered it was unfinished, she knew the task of completing it rested firmly on her shoulders. And somehow the ideas and the words for the rest of the story began to pour into her mind. She's been writing ever since.

It wasn't until another thirteen years later, however, that the romantic in her geared her toward romance. She now focuses on heartwarming multicultural romance with enough passion to enthrall readers who want a little sizzle with their romance. She lives in her native country, Ghana, which provides the exotic setting for most of her novels.